THE LAWYER'S MAIL ORDER DESTINY

IRON CREEK BRIDES

BOOK ELEVEN

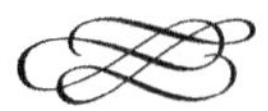

KARLA GRACEY

Published by Beldene Publishing

This book is dedicated to all of my faithful readers, without whom I would be nothing. I thank you for the support, reviews, love, and friendship you have shown me as we have gone through this journey together. I am truly blessed to have such a wonderful readership.

CHARACTER LIST

- **Emily Watson**
- **Richard Ball – lawyer.**
- Mr. Briggs – Emily's mother's landlord in Boston
- Harriet Tolman – a friend of Emily's mother who provides a home for Emily. Married to Martyn
- John, Graeme, Fiona, and Evie – Harriet's children
- Marta Pauling – Emily's friend and housemate
- Mrs. Jarnley – boarding house owner in Boston
- Mr. White – Emily and Marta's landlord in Boston
- Father Michael – priest in Boston
- Dr. Galen – doctor in Boston
- Mr. Holton – Marta's boss at the bakery

- Mr. Gregor – Emily's boss at the mill
- Edward and Mary Ball – Richard's aunt and uncle
- Jonny and Cassie Cable – hotelier and wife
- Andrew and Amy Cable – newspaper owner and wife
- Mrs. Cable – the twins' mother
- Mayor Winston – Iron Creek's mayor
- Geoffrey and Jeannie Drayton – Iron Creek's carpenter and wife
- Marjorie – older lady who works in the mill
- Father Paul – priest in Iron Creek
- Nelly Graham – town nurse and owner of a boarding house in Iron Creek
- Garrett and Katy Harding – sheep farmers
- Alec Jenks – Iron Creek's blacksmith
- Dr. Anna Jenks – town physician. Married to Alec Jenks
- Dr. Lancelot – town physician
- Wesley and Clarice Baker – Iron Creek's baker and wife
- Nelson and Bronwen Gustavson – bookstore owner and wife

PROLOGUE

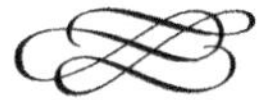

February 13, 1885, Boston, Massachusetts

Upon her return from her mother's funeral, knowing that she was entering the tiny cottage for the last time, Emily Watson felt empty. She took off her coat and hat and hung them on the hook by the door, as she always did, and reached out and touched her mother's threadbare woolen scarf. She buried her head in it, remembering the look on Mom's face when she had given it to her one Christmas so many years ago. Mom had treasured it because it was the first thing Emily had made for her. It made Emily sad knowing Mom would never proudly wrap it around her shoulders, ever again.

With a heavy sigh, Emily turned around. The once warm and loving home felt cold and cramped now. The heavy furniture was too big for the space, and too many things littered every surface. Mom had kept everything Emily had ever brought home, everything she had made, and every ribbon and scrap of lace she had ever worn. There was a lifetime of memories packed in every object, and now she had just a day to pack up every single one of them and leave forever. Where she would go, she did not know.

But that was not their landlord, Mr. Briggs' concern. He wished to continue to make money, and she was in his way. Of course, he had made out that he cared when she had visited his offices in the city to tell him of her mother's passing. He had even offered her the opportunity to remain in the little house at an exorbitant rent a young woman of her age and experience could never have possibly afforded. She simply did not have the funds to do so. And so, from tomorrow, she would be just one of the many homeless people on the streets of Boston.

A knock on the door made her heart jump almost out of her chest. What if he had come to throw her out early? She opened the door cautiously and sighed loudly when she saw the concerned face of her mother's oldest friend, Harriet Tolman. "You didn't stop and talk to anyone after the funeral. Is everything okay?"

"I just wanted to be alone for a while," Emily said, trying hard not to cry. She did not need anyone's pity. "Since Mom passed away, I feel like I've not had a moment to myself, and there is still so much to be done."

Harriet peered around her at the piles Emily had been

sorting through. "Briggs has given you notice?" Harriet asked softly.

It was couched as a question, but Emily knew that Harriet already knew the answer. She nodded and sighed. "I have until the morning."

"Then we'd best get busy," Harriet said. Shc took off her coat, rolled up her sleeves, and came inside. "You sort things, I'll pack them. And you're coming to stay with me, whether you like it or not."

"I can't impose," Emily protested. "You have four children to feed as it is."

"And I cannot tell you how much I would appreciate a little help with them, and with the rent," Harriet said practically.

"I'll find somewhere else as soon as I can," Emily said firmly. "I'll not be a burden."

"No, my love, you'll never be that no matter how long you stay. I loved your mother like a sister. She'd come back and haunt me if I don't take care of you now. Now, what do you need me to do?"

"I couldn't sleep, so I made a start last night. There is nothing in the back room I need to keep," Emily said sadly. "But those piles on the kitchen table are to go with me. The ones in the basket by the fire are to be thrown away."

Harriet began to deftly fold the clothes on the table and put them into a large carpetbag. The two women worked in silence for some time, and before long, the kitchen was sorted, packed, and cleared. They moved upstairs, into the room where Emily's mother had slept. It made her cry to sort through her meager belongings, just a few dresses that had been hemmed and trimmed more times than Emily could count. She checked under the bed, where she found a large wooden box. She pulled it out and wiped the dust off the top of it.

"What's that?" Harriet asked.

"I don't know. I don't remember ever seeing it before," Emily said, lifting the lid. Inside she found several letters, some scraps of ribbon and lace, a few cheap pieces of jewelry that she had only the vaguest memories of her mother wearing, and a gentleman's pocket watch. She took it out of the box and opened it. Three letters were inscribed in a looping italic on the cover. *L.J.W.* It was clearly well-cared for and must have been expensive, yet she had never seen it before. And it must have meant something quite considerable to Mom, given she had kept it through all manner of hard times. "Do you think this was my father's?" she asked Harriet, showing it to her.

Harriet sucked in her breath. "Oh my, I didn't know she still had that." She shook her head. "She swore to me that she sold it years ago."

"Well, either she pawned it and bought it back or she lied to you. It was his, wasn't it?" She knew she sounded angry, but she couldn't help it. The thought that her mother had kept such a memento, given the way her father had left Mom alone with a child to raise, was infuriating.

"It was," Harriet said softly. "She swore she was over him so many times."

"Obviously not," Emily said drily. "Though why she cared for a man who deserted her when she needed him most will remain a mystery to me."

"Don't judge her too harshly. She did the best for you that she could, Em. Heaven knows she had no help from your father or his people."

"So why did she keep this?" Emily demanded. "She let us go hungry rather than sell this."

"I can't answer that, love, but the heart is a funny thing. It's harder than you might think to just turn off your feelings and let someone go."

"Did you know him?" Emily asked. She went back to sorting through the piles of papers her mother had just stuffed into the large wooden box Emily had found under the bed.. "Mom never said anything about him, right up until the day she died. Did you ever meet him? Did she tell you anything about him?"

"I did meet him once. He was at the university," Harriet said sadly. "She said that he loved her and that his family didn't approve. He promised her that it didn't matter. They were wed. I was there. I watched them make their vows, and I would swear that he meant every word. Then, just after she found out you were on your way, he was gone. She never heard anything from him again."

"So, he was a coward when it really came down to it?"

"I suppose he was," Harriet said. "But I've never been sure that your mother even told him you were on your way. I think he truly meant to do right by her. He was a kind man, gentle, sweet. But something made him leave."

"Do you know where he was from?"

"No, Em. I'm sorry. I really don't know much more than what I've told you."

"Did you at least know his name?"

"Logan, I think. But for the life of me, I can't remember his surname."

Emily pulled out a pile of letters addressed to her mother. The handwriting was a youthful scrawl. She flicked through them and noticed each of them was signed with a large *L*. She sank down against the bed and began to read them. They had clearly been written not long after he and her mother had met. They were full of protestations of love and little tidbits about his life before coming to Boston, though not once did he say where he had been raised. She put them aside. It made her sick to her stomach to think that someone could have laid claim to all those feelings of love and yet still abandon her mother, and her, without a backward glance.

She wanted to burn every one of them, but as she took the rubbish downstairs and went to put them in the stove, she found that just like her mother, she was unable to do so. She tucked the letters into the carpetbag along with the pocket watch and her mother's cheap jewelry and wondered what it would be like if she found her father after all these years. Who was he? What did he look like now? What kind of man had he become? And most importantly, why had he left them?

She doubted that she would ever have the answers she needed to make sense of how she had been brought into this world. Mom had never spoken of her father, not even to criticize him for leaving them. Yet she had kept this box full of trinkets and letters from him. Emily wondered how many nights her mother had sat at the kitchen table and read through them all as she polished his watch. It was clear that Mom had never forgotten him. It would be too sad if she had never stopped loving him as well.

She and Harriet loaded her things into a handcart that Emily pushed down the street to Harriet's house. "What do you need of these things?" Harriet asked. Emily pointed at the carpetbag and a small box. "I'll get Martyn to put the rest of your things away in the wood store."

"Thank you," Emily said, picking up the carpetbag. Harriet took the box, then led her upstairs and pointed her toward a solid-looking ladder at the end of the narrow passageway. "It's not much, but I thought you might appreciate a little privacy," she said. She took a couple of steps up the ladder and put the box on the floor above her head, then reached out to Emily. "Give me your things."

Emily handed over the carpetbag, and Harriet put that in the attic before climbing the rest of the way up. Emily followed her a little cautiously. She'd never been that comfortable on a ladder. She didn't trust anything that moved under her as she walked upon it. She glanced around the space as she climbed the final few rungs. It was a little awkward, and she would have to mind her head, but it was clear that Harriet had done all she could to make the attic feel as cozy and welcoming as possible A large trunk had been placed at the end of a comfortable-looking wooden-framed bed with a well-covered straw mattress. The sheets on the bed were spotlessly white. Harriet had even put a small vase of dried flowers on a small table beside the bed.

"I know it isn't what you're used to, but I hope it will do," Harriet said.

"It is more than I could ever have expected," Emily said.

"I'm glad you like it." Harriet beamed. "I shall leave you to get yourself settled in. We will see you downstairs for supper in an hour or so."

"Thank you."

Left alone, Emily picked up the box and took it to the bed. She sat down and opened the lid. She took out the watch and stared at the initials on its case for a long time. Who was her father? Why had Mom kept everything he'd given to her? Why had she never let anyone else into her heart? She picked up the letters and started to read them. The writing was a little difficult to read, but once she got used to it, Emily found herself admiring the beautiful things that her father had written. He had clearly cared very deeply for her mother. Either that or he was a very fluent liar. But rather than answering her questions, she found that it only made her wonder even more why he had left.

CHAPTER 1

May 15, 1889, Boston, Massachusetts

The photograph of Emily and her mother stood proudly on the mantel in Emily's new home. They had saved up for months for it, and it had been taken just a month before Mom's passing. Now, it was Emily's most treasured possession, and it brought back memories of a very special day. They had dressed up in their finest Sunday dresses and visited the photographer's studio just before lunch. The poor photographer had been quite frustrated with them as they simply couldn't stop giggling. He kept begging them to be solemn, but he eventually had to accept that their portrait would be a smiling one.

As they had made their way home, Mom had suddenly grabbed Emily's hand and dragged her into the lobby of one of Boston's finest hotels, where they were greeted by a livery-clad gentleman who showed them to a table in the restaurant. Despite Emily's protests that they would never be able to afford to dine there, Mom had hushed her and placed the thick linen napkin in her lap as though she had been born to such a life. Emily had copied her, still protesting. The lunch had been the most exquisite meal of Emily's life, and Mom had been so proud that she had kept the treat a secret from her.

Now that she knew a little more about her father, Emily couldn't help wondering if such meals had been a part of her mother's life with him. Had he taken her out to such places often? Mom had certainly acted as though being in such a dining room was perfectly normal for her. It broke Emily's heart that she was unable to ask Mom all the questions she had been left with. Not that her mother would have answered them. Whenever Emily had asked about her father, Mom had clammed up and changed the subject quickly.

"We shall miss you," Harriet said a little sadly, carrying some of Emily's things into the tiny cottage that Emily would be sharing with her friend, Marta Pauling. Their new landlord, Mr. White had been recommended to them by Marta's former landlady, Mrs. Jarnley. Marta was due to arrive at any moment.

"And I shall miss you all, too," Emily said, hugging Harriet after she had set down her bags. "But this will be the best for all of us. John and Graeme have grown so much, and Fiona and Evie are young women now. They need their own space, not sharing with their messy and loud brothers."

"And it is closer to the mill," Harriet said, rolling her eyes. "I know, and you will have a wonderful time living with Marta."

Emily laughed. She knew there was no argument she could make that would ever convince Harriet that it was a good thing that she wished to move out of her home. But the little house was bursting at the seams now that the children were all that bit older and much bigger. The lack of space had begun to cause friction, and Emily felt guilty having the attic to herself when Harriet's four children were sharing a single room.

"I will visit often, and you are welcome here whenever you need some peace," she told Harriet as Marta entered the kitchen carrying a large basket covered with a linen cloth.

"You're here," she said delightedly. "I wasn't sure if I would be back in time to be here to meet you. We closed the shop a little late, so I've not had time to go and fetch my things from Mrs. Jarnley's."

"We only just arrived," Emily assured her. "You only just missed Mr. White. He seems very kind and even helped us to bring in some of my things."

"He's a good man. I think he is sweet on Mrs. Jarnley, but she is still in mourning for her husband, though he passed away many years ago now. She thinks he'll treat us fairly, and the rent he's charging us is very reasonable for such a house."

"It really is," Harriet said, nodding. "I was so relieved to see that it is clean and that there's no damp or broken windows. The chimney pulls well, so you'll have no problems with that. There's nothing worse than a fireplace belching smoke."

Emily and Marta shared a quick smile. Emily had warned her friend of how worried Harriet had been about her moving out and what such a low rent might mean for them. She had inspected every inch of the house as soon as Mr. White had given them the keys. Emily had seen her visibly relax once she had done so. Her shoulders had dropped, and her pursed lips and furrowed brow had eased. She still wasn't happy, but she was at least reassured that Emily and Marta would not die in their beds from a badly banked fire.

"How was it at the bakery this morning?" Emily asked.

"Busy," Marta said. She put the basket down on the table and removed the cloth, then pulled out some bread, a meat pie, and a small cake from its depths. "But I managed to get these for us."

"Mmm," Emily said, sniffing the meat pie, which was still warm. "You see, Harriet, I shall be quite alright here."

"You can't expect Marta to steal food from her workplace every day," Harriet said a little brusquely.

"I didn't steal them," Marta bristled. "Mr. Holton was happy to let me have them as a gift to bless our new home."

Harriet shook her head and sank down onto the rocking chair by the stove. "I am sorry, Marta. I should not have said that. I know you would not steal. I am out of sorts. I have been for months. And I shall miss Emily so very much."

"We are only two streets away," Emily said kneeling down in front of Harriet. "And if you need some time to yourself, I will gladly mind the children for you. Send them to us for their dinner every Wednesday if you want."

"I cannot do that," Harriet protested. "That is your afternoon off work. You need it to rest yourself."

"I have all day Sunday to do that," Emily said with a smile. "I love them as if they were my own sisters and brothers so, you send them, or I'll be knocking on your door to fetch them every Wednesday afternoon."

Harriet smiled weakly and patted Emily's cheek. "You are a good girl."

"It is the very least I can do, given everything you have done for me."

"You owe us nothing. We were glad to have you – and you have more than paid your way, bringing in your rent money and helping with the children. You didn't need to do any of that."

"My mom raised me to give back at least as much as has been given to me," Emily said. "I'd have been disrespecting her to do any less. Now, we owe each other nothing at all, so I will invite myself to lunch with you every Sunday and you will send the children here every Wednesday, and that is final."

While they were talking, Marta had quietly gone about preparing the meat pie for their lunch. She had cut it and placed the portions on plates she found in one of Emily's boxes. "Come and eat," she said.

"Yes," Emily said. She stood up and offered a hand to Harriet. "And once we have eaten, we can escort you home, Harriet, then go and fetch your things, Marta."

Some hours later, Marta and Emily sat quietly in front of the fire in their tiny parlor. It had been a long day, but Emily was sure that they were finally settled. Everything had been unpacked and they had found sufficient room in the cupboards in the kitchen for her mother's pots and pans, cutlery, and crockery. Marta had nothing like that. She had been living in a boarding house since she'd come to Boston from her uncle's farm near Medford. They had met at church, where they both helped with the little ones, keeping them occupied while their parents took communion. They had known each other for just five months, but they had become fast friends and found that they had much in common.

Marta had also lost her mother a few years ago and, like Emily, had also not known her father. She did at least know who he was, though. Frederick Pauling had sadly died from an accident on his brother's farm, not long after Marta had turned five years old. She had also felt herself to be a burden on her uncle and his family, as Emily felt herself to be on Harriet and hers. Marta had come to Boston after securing a job at Holton's bakery, and while she had been quite comfortable at Mrs. Jarnley's boarding house, it was more expensive than she could afford. As they had both complained about their situations, it had grown clear to them what they should do about it.

"Who would have thought that girls like us would have a home like this?" Marta said happily.

"I certainly never did," Emily admitted. "I assumed I would need to marry to even consider it."

"I can hardly believe that Mrs. Jarnley suggested us to Mr. White. After all, it leaves her a boarder short."

"I doubt she'll have an empty room for long. Her boarding house is one of the nicest in the city."

They sat quietly for a moment, both watching the flames flickering in the grate. Emily was grateful for the peace and quiet of the little house. As much as she loved Harriet's family, their home was never silent. There was always someone shouting, arguing, or clumping up and down the stairs. It was strange to not hear anything other than the sounds of the fire crackling and the occasional clip-clop of a horse's hooves on the cobbles outside.

"What would you have done if you had not found the position at Holton's?" Emily asked her friend. She had often wondered what her future might hold, knowing that at some point she would have to stop relying upon Harriet's generosity. But she had never come to a decision about what that might look like. In a way, most of her curiosity had been caught up with trying to understand why her mother had remained in love with a man who had left her when she needed him most. Her past echoed loudly, often drowning out what might be her future.

"I suppose I would have had to find a husband," Marta said. "My uncle wanted me to marry one of the men who worked on the farm."

"And you didn't want that?"

"I didn't want the man he had in mind," Marta said with a wry smile. "He was a cruel man who often beat the animals on the farm. Always angry. I don't doubt that he would have beaten me, too."

Emily shuddered. "I think that you were right not to settle for such a man."

"What would you have done, do you think, if Mrs. Tolman had not taken you in?"

Emily sighed. "I have no idea," she admitted. "I didn't have time to make a plan. I am so grateful to her for being there for me. My mom would be so grateful to her."

"I thought about becoming a mail-order bride," Marta said with a chuckle. "But what if the man at the end of the letter turned out to be even more cruel than the man I was running from?"

"A mail-order bride?" Emily asked. She'd never heard of such a thing.

"You see the advertisements in the newspapers all the time," Marta explained. "Men all over the country looking for a wife. You've never seen them?"

"I don't think I've ever even read a newspaper. They weren't something we had in the house. Mom liked dime novels. I think she preferred to escape her life rather than read about how dreadful the world was."

Marta jumped up. "Wait here," she said. She hurried out to the kitchen and reappeared moments later with a newspaper in her hand. She flicked through the pages, then gave it to Emily. "See," she said, pointing at an entire page of advertisements. The heading at the top of the page read *Matrimonials*.

"Well, I never," Emily said after reading a couple of the advertisements. Some were quite sad, others were jollier, but some just sounded desperate. "I can hardly believe that people do this."

"I think some do it because they are lonely," Marta said kindly. "But others, probably because they have no other choice open to them."

The clock on the mantel that Marta had brought with her chimed softly nine times. "I should go to bed," Marta said. "I would normally have been fast asleep by now."

"Go, you have to be up early," Emily encouraged her.

Marta yawned, stretched, and nodded. "Good night, Emily," she said.

"Good night."

Left alone, Emily continued to read the advertisements in the newspaper. A few were simply from men who wished to find a wife, while others were lengthy and went into great detail about what they expected and what they might offer. Some were so boastful that she could hardly believe they could be in any way truthful. But others were humble, even endearing, and she could understand why women with no other hope might respond to those. She was even surprised to see that some advertisements had been placed by women looking for husbands. Such forward behavior seemed wrong to Emily, though she knew that many needed to take drastic actions. But surely such women would be unlikely to get men responding to them? Men, in her experience – limited though that was – seemed to expect women to raise babies and work hard but not to have opinions or any kind of personal initiative.

But the more of the advertisements she read, the more she wanted to respond to one of them. Not because she had any particular urge to be wed, but out of interest, to find out what manner of men had actually placed such advertisements. She wouldn't do it, of course. It would not be fair to lead a man on, then dash his hopes when he found out that she had never been serious about marriage from the start. But then, she saw one advert that seemed a little different from the others.

Gentleman Lawyer of Boston. Gentle, kindly, too busy to socialize, but can offer interesting correspondence. Seeks a young woman with interests in music, literature, and theater to write to regularly. Responses to Box 3145, The Boston Times

He didn't seem to be looking for a wife, though his advertisement was on the matrimonials page. And he did not seek to display his wealth or specify what manner of woman he expected to reply, and he was actually here in Boston. Should she write to this gentleman, she might be able to find out more about him, and if they truly got on well, perhaps they might progress to meeting in person.

But she had to acknowledge that her real interest in him was what he might be able to do for her. A lawyer had come to the mill some months earlier, seeking out a young woman who was due an inheritance. He had tracked her down to the mill, having only the smallest of clues to work with. Perhaps Emily might be able to interest this lawyer in helping her find out more about her father, if she could interest him in her past?

She stood up and stepped away from the newspaper. Whatever was she thinking? Such a man would most certainly not consider a mill girl like her, and the only person likely to be interested in finding her father was her. She could not expect a stranger to care enough to devote their time to such a hopeless chase. Especially not a man already too busy to manage a social life given how many opportunities must be open to him as a young professional man. Even if he did have the time, she doubted that a lawyer would want to mix socially with a mill girl. Then again, perhaps he was as different in person as he seemed to be in his advertisement, and such a thing would not matter to him.

As she made to go upstairs to her bed after banking the fire for the night, she realized that she would never know if he did care about such things or whether he might consider helping her if she didn't write to him. She was as deserving and as good a friend as anyone else likely to be reading his advertisement. Besides, if he didn't want to get to know her better, he could always just ignore her letter. She had to take the chance. She would certainly never be likely to meet such a man in real life and could not afford to hire a lawyer herself – and she needed to know who her father was and why he had left.

CHAPTER 2

May 20, 1889, Boston, Massachusetts

The room was dark. The heavy drapes pulled across the large windows blocked out the bright sunshine that made the unexpected carpet of snow on the ground glint and glisten. Richard Ball, a man usually so confident in any situation, suddenly felt anything but brave. He was reluctant to cross the threshold of Uncle Edward's office. Once a place of bustling efficiency, it was now the great man's sickroom. And though Richard knew that death came to every man in time, he had not expected to ever see this day. Men like Uncle Edward did not die so young of cancer or other such mortal maladies. They died on the battlefield, heroically.

A delicate woman with pale skin and vivid blue eyes was sitting by his bedside. Always elegant, always gentle, his

Aunt Mary looked up and saw him hovering in the doorway. She gave him a sad smile, stood up, and beckoned him, forwards. Not wanting to show his fear to her when her own pain and despair must outweigh his one hundred times over, he strode forward and embraced her. He pressed a kiss to her forehead, and she patted his cheek affectionately. "I'm so glad you are here," she said in a whisper. "I think he's been waiting for you."

"I came as soon as I received word," Richard said. "Made the coachman push the horses every mile of the way. I was so afraid I would not make it in time. What happened? I've barely been gone a month. He seemed in perfect health when I left town."

Richard glanced over his aunt's shoulder at the figure lying in the bed. His uncle lay barely moving, his skin sallow, his eyes closed. He had lost a lot of weight and looked almost skeletal. Richard could hardly bear it. How could his uncle have declined so rapidly that he was now so very frail when he had been so strong, so vivid, so much larger than life mere weeks earlier?

Aunt Mary nodded and indicated he should take the chair by the bedside. Richard hesitated before doing so, but she gave him a nod as she perched on the bed beside her husband. "I think he has been keeping his illness quiet for a very long time," she said, frowning down at the sleeping figure slightly. "Perhaps even before he lost his command at

Fort Meade, though he'd never have told anyone about it. He's never been one to complain."

"You believe he knew even then? But he was posted to Fort Bennett for six months before he returned to Boston? Surely, he would not have accepted that command if he knew he was sick?"

"I don't know if he knew he was this sick. Knowing him, he would have believed his will was sufficient to ward any sickness away simply by ignoring it. He wrote to me that he was having stomach pains, but he put it down to the fish supper he'd eaten the night before. He only admitted to me last week that he had not told me how long he'd been having them, or that he had been passing blood."

"And did he seek any treatment?"

"Not until it was too late," Aunt Mary said, shaking her head. "He was always too stubborn for his own good." She leaned over and kissed her husband's slightly clammy forehead. "I shall leave you two for a moment and fetch us both some refreshments."

Richard wanted to beg her not to leave him alone in the room, but he would not let her know how much the figure of his dying uncle disturbed him. If she could bear it, he would do so too. He reached out and took his uncle's hand and pressed it to his cheek. Uncle Edward's skin was cold and the veins on his hands showed through the thinning skin vividly. "Why did you not tell us?" Richard whispered.

"There are doctors who could have helped, surgeons who cut out tumors. It didn't have to be this way."

His uncle's eyes flickered open and he tried to speak, but his once strong, clear voice was so quiet and inarticulate that Richard could barely make out what he was saying. Uncle Edward grew frustrated by this and began to point agitatedly at the desk in the corner of the room. Richard got up and went to the desk. He reached for the drawer, his uncle nodded, tears flooding his rheumy eyes. Inside the drawer, there was a key. It was small and made of brass. It matched the trim on a cabinet behind the desk.

"You want me to open the door?" Richard asked.

Uncle Edward nodded slowly. Richard placed the key in the lock and turned it. The door swung open with a slight creek. Inside the cupboard was a pile of paperwork. Richard took the stack of letters and documents out and took them to the bed. On top was a letter addressed to him. "Shall I read it now?" he asked. Uncle Edward nodded again.

Richard slid a letter knife under the seal and broke it carefully, unfolded the paper, and began to read. He felt tears well up as he read his uncle's words. After his parents' deaths, Aunt Mary and Uncle Edward had taken him in and given him a home. Of course, where that home was had often changed as Uncle Edward's commission in the army had them move from fort to fort, but it had been full of love. They had never been blessed with children of their own, but they had always treated him as if he were their son. When Richard had been offered a place to study law at Harvard, Aunt Mary had insisted that they buy a house in Boston, ostensibly for when Uncle Edward finally left the army. She had even come to live there, though her husband was still serving in South Dakota, to ensure Richard always had a good meal and a comfortable home to return to after the long days in the lecture hall and library.

The letter had obviously been written some months earlier, just after Uncle Richard had finally left the army and come home to spend his final moments on earth with his family. In it, he told Richard all the practical details that would need to be taken care of, where he banked and who to speak to there in order to ensure Aunt Mary would be well provided for. He also praised Richard, as the son of his heart, for the man he had become and thanked him for the care that he would continue to give to Aunt Mary.

"You know I will always make sure she has all she needs," Richard assured his uncle. "The two of you are the only parents I remember, and I cannot thank you both for all you have done for me."

Uncle Edward blinked. He reached for the pile of documents on the bed and managed to slide one out from the rest, and pushed it toward Richard. Richard picked up the thick parchment-like document and broke the wax seal. As he unfolded it, he realized it was his uncle's will. He skimmed it quickly, glad that almost everything had been left to his aunt. But there were a few odd bequests of treasured items that Uncle Edward wanted to be given to specific people.

Uncle Edward reached for Richard's hand as he set it back on top of the pile of papers. "Take them to everyone yourself," he said hoarsely, enunciating each word slowly and carefully, clearly determined to make Richard understand.

"I will, Uncle," Richard promised. "I will."

Uncle Edward passed mere hours later, and Aunt Mary was inconsolable. Richard followed his uncle's orders for his funeral to the letter, ensuring that the deeds of the house were put into Aunt Mary's name and arranging the transfer of his assets to her went smoothly. Richard was reassured to see that Aunt Mary grew stronger with each passing day. She had been used to living without her husband for months on end, but this was different. This time, Uncle Edward would never return to her, so she would have to find her way to him someday. But Uncle Edward had made it quite clear that he did not want either of them to mourn him to the detriment of them living their lives.

As Richard began to prepare for the journey around the country to distribute his uncle's more peculiar bequests, Uncle Edward's hopes for Richard became abundantly clear. A bright, sunny May morning brought a small pile of letters addressed to Richard, all sent to him from *The Matrimonial Times*.

"What is it?" Aunt Mary asked as he entered the dining

room to join her for breakfast. "You have the most peculiar expression on your face."

Richard laughed and waved the letters. "It seems that my dear uncle decided that it was time for me to marry."

"I don't understand," she said, reaching out for the letters. He handed them to her. "But you've not read them. How do you know that they have anything to do with Edward?"

"Look at the return address on the back," he said with a grin, "and then tell me with a straight face that placing an advertisement to find me a bride isn't exactly the sort of thing my dear uncle would have done in his final days."

She turned them over and gasped. "Oh, my! He often said that it was time for you to take a wife, but I can hardly believe that he would go so far as to do this." She put them down beside his place setting while he helped himself to eggs and bacon from the salvers on the buffet behind her. "What will you do about it?"

"I'll ignore them," Richard said simply. "Much as I wish to please my dear uncle, I will not marry some woman I have never met."

"You don't have to marry her before you meet, you simply have to write to her," Aunt Mary pointed out with a grin. It was the first time that Richard had seen her truly amused since his uncle's passing. He was glad that his uncle had unwittingly managed to provide that, at least. But he was not yet ready to take a wife. He had barely finished university and had much to do to establish a reputation as a lawyer before he felt it would be prudent to take a bride.

"I would not wish to toy with a woman's affections," Richard said. "It is better that I never even respond to them. I'll burn them in the fire once I have eaten."

"Think about it on your travels," Aunt Mary said softly. "You might change your mind. Keep them until then."

"So, you wish me to be wed as much as Uncle Edward did?" Richard said, giving her an indulgent smile.

"You are a fine young man, polite and with a good future ahead of you. If your uncle's untimely demise shows anything at all, then it must be that life is short and it is wise to take chances when they arise, is it not?"

"It could be considered that way, I suppose."

"But you still have no intention of writing to any of these young ladies?" Aunt Mary said with a giggle. She reached for the letters and tucked them into the pocket of her apron. "I will take good care of these, just in case you change your mind."

"I will not," he assured her as he finished his breakfast.

After eating, Richard ran up the stairs to fetch his bags. He quickly checked that he had all the items his uncle had wanted him to distribute and the railway tickets that would take him to the first recipient on the list. Once he was sure that he had everything he needed, he made his way back downstairs. Aunt Mary was standing by the open front door. Through it, he could see the carriage waiting at the roadside.

"Are you sure you will be alright without me?" he asked his aunt as he embraced her.

"I will," she promised him. "Your uncle wanted you to be the one to take the news of his passing to his friends and give them his final gifts. It would be selfish of me to keep you here when such an important task must be undertaken."

"I will be back before you know it, and I will write every week," he promised her as he bent down so she might kiss his cheek. "And I have arranged for Aunt Deborah to come and keep you company. She'll be here shortly."

"You did not need to do that," Aunt Mary assured him, "but I will be glad of her company. The house is always a little too big and a lot too empty when you are not in it, my boy." She squeezed him tightly one more time, then stepped away. She waited on the step as he got into the carriage and waved him off, tears rolling down her cheeks.

CHAPTER 3

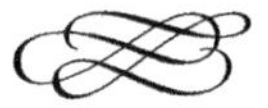

August 1, 1889, Iron Creek, Minnesota

Richard walked out of the station building and onto the street. He looked around him. He didn't know what he had been expecting, but it wasn't what he saw. Carriages and wagons rumbled past him, people scurried cheerfully about their business, and everybody seemed to have time to stop and chat for a few moments, no matter how speedily they had been moving beforehand. A few people even waved at him or doffed their caps as they drove past. It wasn't a vast city, but it was certainly a town doing well. He smiled and decided that he liked Iron Creek.

A smart gig was waiting outside the station house. Richard approached it. A well-dressed man stood at the pony's head, scratching around the animal's ears as it dipped its nose into a feed bag. "Could you give me directions to Pinewood Lodge, please?"

"Better still, I can take you there," the man said, reaching out a hand to Richard. "You're Richard Ball, right?" Richard nodded as he took the man's hand and shook it firmly. "Jonny Cable, hotelier and the man that you're here to meet."

"You received my telegrams," Richard said, feeling relieved that he would not have to explain his presence here. He'd had to do so too many times on his whirlwind tour of the country, bestowing his uncle's bequests.

"We did. And a number of letters that Mrs. Ball sent on for you." Mr. Cable handed him a stack of letters, tied neatly with string.

"She's very efficient, Aunt Mary," Richard said with a wry smile as he flicked through them, noting they all came from the newspaper. She was about as subtle as Uncle Edward had been about his need to find a bride. He stuffed them in his pocket with a shake of his head. Mr. Cable raised a single eyebrow quizzically, but he did not press the matter when he received no explanation.

Instead, he took Richard's bag and stowed it carefully under the bench of the gig. "Andy and I, we're sorry for your loss," Mr. Cable said solemnly as he indicated Richard should get in. "I know we sent her a letter at the time of Major Ball's passing, but when you return, please pass on our condolences to your aunt. She is a fine woman."

"Yes, she is," Richard agreed, clambering aboard. "The finest."

Mr. Cable removed the nose bag from around the pony's neck and stowed it under the driver's bench, then climbed up himself. He clicked to the pony, and without even a touch of the long driver's whip, the gig began to move steadily forward.

"The town is bigger than I expected," Richard said as they made their way along Main Street, before turning up onto the road that would lead them to the hotel. "Uncle Edward often complained bitterly that his favorite officers had deserted him to move to a frozen one-horse town in Minnesota."

Mr. Cable laughed at that. "I can just imagine him saying that," he said fondly. "And to be honest with you, Iron Creek was just a staging post really, until about ten years ago. It's been steadily growing since then, and it boomed once the railroad came through."

"I don't think he ever quite understood that anything or anywhere was better than being a soldier."

"Oh, I think he did," Mr. Cable said with a sad smile. "He spoke often of you and your aunt. I think he would have loved to have given it all up and gone to Boston to be with you both. But his sense of duty was very strong. He was the finest officer I ever served under."

"I didn't know that he ever thought about a different life, one away from the army," Richard said. "I will be sure to tell

Aunt Mary, I think it would bring her comfort to know that he spoke of us when we were apart. Thank you for that, Mr. Cable."

"Jonny," he said firmly. "And he spoke of you both, all the time. He was so proud of you when you finished university. Bored us rigid with it." The two men laughed.

"He spoke of you, your brother, and the regiment when he was with us. He was proud of all you achieved, too. He was worried half out of his mind about Andrew and his injuries during that terrible ambush."

"We all were, but it's a testament to Andy's character that he found a way to be just as successful without the use of his legs as he was with them." Jonny chuckled. "He's happier than he's ever been. And as you found it comforting to know he talked of you, it is good to know he thought of us at all – even if, perhaps, you would have rather he had spoken of other things than us when he was with you. He was a fine commanding officer and a good friend."

They drove in silence for a while, both lost in their memories. Richard looked around at the trees lining the mountain road and listened to the birds singing all around them. "It is beautiful here. No wonder you wanted to stay."

"Well, once Andy was injured, it just didn't feel right being in the army."

"You're twins, aren't you?"

"We are. Those few months we were apart were the hardest in my life – but don't tell him that."

"I'm sure he felt the same way," Richard said. "Will he be joining us later?"

"I'll take you to his house for supper this evening," Jonny said. "He wanted to come to the station to meet you but he runs a newspaper, and it is always busy midweek."

"I look forward to meeting him."

The hotel appeared as they turned a corner. Richard whistled his appreciation. "Well, I don't think I was expecting that," he said as they pulled to a halt outside the grand front entrance.

"You thought it would be a log cabin in the woods?" Jonny said, thankfully not taking offense.

"No, but this could rival the finest hotels in the land," Richard said. He got down from the gig and reached for his bag, but Jonny had already lifted it out and indicated that Richard should follow him inside.

"That was my plan," Jonny said. "Who wants to stay in a place with uncomfortable beds, the risk of fleas, and terrible food? Especially in Minnesota in the winter." He laughed.

Richard stared around the entrance hall. It was large, with a double-height ceiling and marble floor. An elegant staircase was set centrally at the opposite end of the vast space. Tables and chairs were dotted around the central space, with large green plants adding a splash of color. All manner of people were sitting drinking coffee, eating cake, and chatting. All walks of life were here, yet it did not take away from the exclusive feel of the grand foyer. Richard loved it. There was no pretension. Simply people being people.

Jonny's eyes scanned the room and stopped on a young man in a dark blue livery who was standing beside the highly polished oak counter. Jonny beckoned the lad to them and handed him Richard's bag. "Fred here will show you to your room," he said. "Get yourself settled, and meet me in the bar," he pointed to a room to the left of the foyer, "at seven."

Richard followed Fred up the grand staircase and along a corridor to a set of double doors. Fred pulled a key from his pocket and turned it in the lock before handing it to Richard, then pushed open the doors and stood back out of the way. Richard stepped into the room. In front of him was a tastefully decorated chamber with a comfortable-looking sofa. A writing desk was set against the wall between the two large windows, a small chair tucked neatly underneath it. Two armchairs sat at either end of the sofa, a low table in front of it.

Fred placed Richard's bag on a table by the door. "Your bedroom is the door to the right, and your bathroom is the door to the left," he said, indicating the almost invisible doors at the far left of the room. "Would you like me to light your fire?"

"No, I'm quite warm enough thank you, but could you have some hot water sent up so that I might have a wash?"

Fred moved to the door to the left and opened it. "Sir, your bathroom has hot water," he said with a grin.

"Well, I'll be..." Richard said, rubbing at his chin as he stepped into the bathroom and began to turn the taps.

"We've all the conveniences here, Sir," Fred said. "Mr. Cable said he wanted to compete with the finest hotels in Boston and New York, Sir."

"Well, I think he has outdone most of them with this," Richard said. "I knew such things exist, but I have never seen one before."

"Would you like help to unpack, Sir?"

"No, I think I can manage," Richard said, moving back into the comfortable parlor and looking at the solitary bag on the table. Fred bobbed his head politely, left, and shut the doors behind him.

Richard opened his bag and started to put his things away in the grand chest of drawers beside the table. He had to smile as he did so. He had left Boston with two trunks full of things that he had given to the people Uncle Richard had wanted to have them. There were just two items left to give away, and they would be gone tonight.

Some of the bequests had been quite logical. Giving Uncle Edward's dueling pistols to the man he had once threatened with a duel to claim Aunt Mary's hand, for example. Aunt Mary had put a stop to such nonsense and had told both men firmly that she would choose her future, that she would not marry just because someone had won her in such a terrible way. The two men had gone on to become good friends, even after Aunt Mary had made her choice. Reginald Walters had shed a tear when Richard had handed them to him.

But there had been some bequests that Richard simply had not made sense of. A pair of snowshoes for a man who lived in Florida, and a pair of spectacles for a young woman in Biloxi. He hoped that their relevance made some kind of sense to them, at least, even if they had not wished to share the reasons with him. It had been an interesting trip, but Richard couldn't help being a little grateful that it was nearly finished. He was looking forward to getting home and seeing Aunt Mary. Despite her protestations of being quite well in her letters and telegrams, he was worried that she might not be faring as well as she claimed. He pulled the letters she had forwarded out of his pocket and grinned. She must be well if she was doing such things.

Reluctantly, he untied the string and began to read them. Some were badly written, with poor spelling and grammar but a lot of desperation. Others were boastful, claiming attributes that would make those young women unlikely to need to find a husband via the newspaper. A few made him smile, and he could almost imagine writing back to them. But he knew that he would not. He had no wish to marry. There was still much he had to do to further his career before he could reasonably consider taking a wife.

And then there was a letter that truly intrigued him.

Dear Gentleman Lawyer of Boston,

I am sorry for contacting you this way, but after reading your advertisement in the newspaper, the thought of doing so became quite overpowering. You see, I do not wish to write to you with a view to marriage – though your words did not necessarily imply that you were looking for a wife, anyway. I do hope you will not think me impertinent for approaching you in this manner.

You see, I have no money to pay a Boston lawyer such as yourself, but I have a dilemma that can, perhaps, only be solved by such a man. All I ask is that you read my story before dismissing me out of hand, if that is not too much to ask?

My mother passed away four years ago, leaving me alone in the world. I never knew my father, and she never spoke of him much. However, when we went through her things, I found a box that contained a few letters and a pocket watch that belonged to him, bearing an inscription of his initials inside. I found it perplexing that she would have kept such trinkets if she believed him to have left us willingly – as I must confess, I always assumed he must have done.

Yet, despite all manner of hardships that we faced over the years, she kept this watch, despite its obvious value. She kept his letters and must have read them many times as the paper is fragile, stained a little, and easy to rip from all the times they have been folded and unfolded.

Her oldest and dearest friend, who kindly took me in

after my mother passed away, said that she was there when Mom married the man who was my father, but that his family did not approve of the match. She always assumed that they had insisted on an annulment or some such so that he might be free of my mother. But she was sure that he loved Mom and admitted to being very surprised when he left.

And so, I find myself puzzled. I thought his identity did not matter to me, that Mom's love was all I needed. But I know that I have been fooling myself. I need to know why he left us, and why he never even wrote to Mom again after he disappeared, to at least explain why he had gone.

As I said above, I do not have money to pay a fancy lawyer to track him down. I work in Gregor's mill, near the Boston docks. I have a regular wage and will gladly pay you a little each week if you could perhaps spare the time to try to track him down for me? I do understand if such a thing is asking too much of you. But I have to ask. I hope you can understand that.

Yours most hopefully

Emily Watson

CHAPTER 4

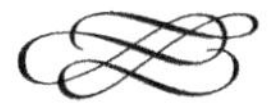

August 1, 1889, Iron Creek, Minnesota

Normally, such a request would be met with short shrift. The partners at the law firm he had been taken on by after his graduation would frown upon such tasks. Grantley, Bedford, and Chesterton did not stoop to locating missing persons. Their clientele was wealthy and required assistance in managing their estates – not chasing after wayward fathers. But though he knew he had been blessed to be offered a position in their hallowed halls, Richard often found practicing law there to be a stuffy and dull profession.

But Miss Watson was offering him a chance at a little excitement and the chance to use his research skills in a way that would offer a real person some real peace of mind. Hastily, he wrote back to her. When he read the letter back, he realized that all he had written was a barrage of questions.

He shook his head and began to draft it again. When he was done, he sealed it and addressed it. He would give it to Fred or to Jonny and ask them to mail it for him.

The chime of the clock, for the quarter hour, made him look up. He could hardly believe that it was already a quarter past six. He took a quick soak in the bath, marveling at the speed that the tub filled with hot water, then dressed for dinner. He ran down the stairs and reached the foyer as the grand clock on the wall struck seven o'clock and grinned to himself. There was no sign of Jonny in the bar, so he ordered a brandy. He sipped at it slowly as he looked out of the windows at the mountains while he waited. He watched as an eagle soared overhead, then suddenly swooped down to the ground, and back into the air once more. From so far away, he couldn't see if the eagle had caught anything, but it flew away so Richard could only assume it had been successful.

Jonny arrived at a run, his cheeks flushed, his hair a little mussed. "I am sorry I am late," he puffed. "I was playing with my children and lost track of the time."

"A father should lose track of time when spending time with his children," Richard said with a smile. "Uncle Edward often did the same, playing with me. And I must confess to almost being late myself. I quite lost track of time and had to hurry to get bathed and dressed. I will have to indulge in that glorious tub in my room properly another day."

Jonny chuckled. "The indoor outhouses are a joy, are they not? I cannot tell you how much trouble my decision to have those caused dear Geoffrey, the town carpenter."

"A carpenter?" Richard asked incredulously.

"Yes, one of the finest men I know. I set him the challenge and trusted him to come up with a solution. He designed the entire place after listening to all my demands. The man is a veritable genius."

"I have to agree," Richard said. "I hope I will get to meet him during my stay here."

"I can make sure of it," Jonny said with a smile. "He and his lovely wife Jeannie are a delight. I shall get Cassie to invite them for supper one night. How long do you intend to stay here with us?"

"As my travels progressed, I must admit that I was looking forward to getting back to Boston, but now that I am here, I must confess to wanting to explore this place more with every minute I stay here."

Jonny laughed and clapped him on the back. "Iron Creek is like that."

They finished their drinks and made their way outside. The sun was getting lower in the sky, but sunset would be some time away yet. Richard imagined that sunsets must be rather spectacular, bathing the mountains and trees in a soft, orangey-pink glow. He looked forward to seeing it immensely.

"Do you ride?" Jonny asked. "I can get the gig out, but it is a lovely evening. It might be nicer to ride."

"I love to ride, and that is a wonderful idea," Richard agreed. "I haven't had a chance to have a good gallop since leaving Boston."

Jonny led them around the back of the hotel to the stables. A neat, cobbled yard was enclosed on three sides by wooden stalls. Horses of all sizes and colors nodded and nickered at the sight of them. A young lad in short breeches and a flat cap was lying on a bale of straw, but he jumped to his feet as soon as he saw Jonny. "Sorry, Sir," he said, his cheeks flushing red at being caught napping.

"It's late, Sam, and you've been here since dawn. Go home and get a good night's sleep," Jonny said kindly.

"But you need horses, and it's my job," Sam said anxiously.

"I think that between the two of us," Jonny winked at Richard, "we can saddle a couple of horses. After all, we've been doing it longer than you've been alive, both of us."

Sam smiled, doffed his cap, and didn't wait to be reassured again. He ran off toward the track that led to Iron Creek without a backward glance.

"He's a good lad and works hard," Jonny said, letting himself into one of the nearby stalls. He led a handsome chestnut mare out and handed the lead rein to Richard. "This is Bemised. It means 'one who flies' in the language of the

Ojibwe, the tribe that lives in the valley. If you want a gallop, she is the fastest in our stables."

"She is beautiful," Richard said, running a hand along the muscular flanks of the mare while Jonny grabbed a saddle. Richard took it from him and got Bemised ready while Jonny fetched a dappled gray, saddled her, and leaped onto her back. Richard put his foot in the stirrup and bounced into the saddle, crooning to Bemised as he did so.

They walked out of the stable yard and onto the road down to Iron Creek, but instead of staying on it, Jonny led the way into the neighboring meadow and gave his mount a gentle nudge. Bemised needed no encouragement and was soon galloping after the gray. In no time at all, she was out in front. Richard felt all his worries and concerns dissipate as he felt the strong muscles bunching and releasing underneath him and the wind in his hair. He slowed a little as they reached the trees bordering the meadow, letting Jonny catch him up and lead them through the woodland.

By the time they reached Andrew's home, Richard felt refreshed and alive, ready for anything. After he had dismounted and hitched Bemised to the fence, he tapped his jacket pocket. They were still there. The ride had not dislodged the gifts his uncle had wished him to deliver to Iron Creek. He had no clue why his uncle wanted them given to the Cable twins, as had been the case for so many of his uncle's bequests, but he was glad that he had been able to honor his uncle one last time by doing this for him.

The door opened as they reached the bottom of the steps up to the porch. A young woman, who Richard assumed must be Amy Cable, smiled at them. "Your supper's on the stove. Andy's in his study," she said. She stood up on her tiptoes and kissed Jonny on the cheek before turning to Richard and giving him a warm smile. "You must be Mr. Ball. I am so sorry for your loss. Andy talks of your uncle in such glowing terms. I wish I could have met him."

"Please call me Richard," he assured her. "I know my uncle was happy to hear Andrew had found someone who made him happy. He always felt guilty about Andrew's injuries."

"Andy would have told him there was no need," Mrs. Cable said with a smile. "At least, once he came to terms with them. And you must call me Amy if we are to be informal tonight."

"No need to feel guilty at all," a deep voice confirmed from behind her. She stood aside, and Richard could see a man who was the very image of his brother but in a wheeled chair rolling himself toward the door. "It took me far too long to stop feeling sorry for myself and realize I still had much to live for. Thank heavens for matrimonial advertisements." He winked at Jonny, who grinned and glanced at Richard.

Feeling a little self-conscious, Richard wondered if Jonny had perhaps told his brother of the letters that Aunt Mary had forwarded. Were they teasing him, or was he being genuine? Richard turned back to Amy. "You met because of an advertisement?"

"We did," Amy said proudly.

"As did half the town," Jonny joked.

"Really?" Richard asked, his eyes wide.

"Virtually every wedding that has happened in Iron Creek in the past ten years only happened because of the matrimonials pages," Amy said with a grin.

"Even you?" Richard asked Jonny.

"Especially me," Jonny said proudly. "Cassie is the best thing that ever happened to me, though I only started to write to her after I stopped receiving letters from my dear sister-in-law when she stopped being my brother's nurse and became his wife."

"Neither of you intended marriage?"

"Not in the slightest," Andy said. "When my dear brother placed the advertisement for me, I was so full of self-pity that I would never have thought that anyone could ever find it in them to love me."

"Yet you both found love?"

The twins nodded. "You should answer a couple of those letters. You never know where it might lead," Jonny said with a grin.

Richard fingered the letter in his pocket that he had meant to give to Jonny to mail, wondering if he should actually send it after all. He truly wasn't looking for love. But Miss Watson needed his help. He couldn't let her down. But he could not bear the teasing he knew would likely come if the twins thought he was trying to find a wife.

"Well, as pleasant as this is, I must get going." Amy gave her husband a lingering kiss before picking up a basket. "I will be back in three hours."

"You aren't staying?" Richard asked.

"I think it wise to leave you three to talk alone. I do not want you to think you have to include me when you will all enjoy your reminiscing much more without me to worry about. And I have a story to investigate."

With that, she left them alone on the porch. Andrew beckoned them inside. Jonny led the way to the kitchen. A large pine table stood in the center of the room, laid with three sets of knives, forks and glasses.

"Have a seat," Jonny said, pointing to one of the two settings where there was a chair. "I'll serve us some food."

"Are you sure I can't help?" Richard asked, as Andrew rolled into the kitchen.

"No, everything is organized. My wife would have been a real asset in a military campaign," Andrew joked. He wheeled himself into the larder at the back of the kitchen and emerged with three plates on his lap and a large bottle of beer. He placed the beer on the table and handed his brother the plates. Jonny lifted the lid from a pot on the stove and began to ladle hot stew onto the plates while Andrew wheeled himself up to the place setting where there was no chair and poured the beer.

The food was excellent, and it wasn't long before the three men were sharing stories about Uncle Edward. Richard had to admit that talking with the twins was the most cathartic experience of his journey. They talked about the Uncle Edward he knew, the brave, loyal soldier who would lay down his life for country, regiment, and his loved ones. When they had finished the meal, he pulled out the two small packages from his pocket and handed them to each of the brothers. "I do not know what is inside," he admitted. "Every bequest on this journey of mine has been as much of a surprise to me as it has to the recipients. Uncle Edward wrapped each one before he got too sick."

The twins looked at each other briefly, then opened the packages. It amused Richard to see that they did so in exactly the same way, at exactly the same pace. And so, they both found out what they had been left by Uncle Edward together. And as they both saw their own bequest, and each other's, they burst out laughing. "Tiepins," they said in unison, shaking their heads.

"I don't understand," Richard said. "Why would he give you tiepins?"

"Because he knew we hated wearing ties," the twins said together.

"I always knew that he knew that we used our tiepins to pick the locks of the food store," Andy said thoughtfully.

"Yet he never once reprimanded us for it," Jonny added. "He was a sly one, sometimes."

Richard grinned. It was possibly the most amusing of his uncle's bequests, and one that was obviously much appreciated by the recipients.

"Thank you for this," Andy said, a tear in his eye. "He was one of the finest men I have ever known."

Jonny nodded, but none of them spoke again for a few moments, each of them lost in memories of the man they had all lost too soon. Richard couldn't help feeling a real kinship with these young men. His uncle's bequests had introduced him to all manner of people, but he couldn't help thinking that there was a reason why Uncle Edward had insisted this visit be the last one that he would make. He wanted Richard to have time to get to know the young men he had taken under his wing, just as much as he had done with Richard.

And now he was here, Richard wanted that, too. That didn't mean that his uncle was right about everything, but he couldn't help thinking that without realizing it, his uncle's advertisement might actually have been for the best, too. He would not find a bride that way, as the twins had done – of that he was certain – but he might just find his love for his work again.

CHAPTER 5

September 3, 1889, Boston, Massachusetts

"There's a letter here for you, Em," Marta called. Emily had been dozing on her bed and half jumped out of her skin at the sound of her friend's voice.

"A letter?" she called back, sitting up and shaking her head, trying to get rid of the groggy feeling she was always left with when she fell asleep in the daytime.

Marta appeared in the doorway. "Yes, come all the way from Minnesota," she said. "At least, I think that's the furthest away of all these stamps." She handed Emily the letter. Almost every bit of the envelope was covered in stamps from the postal offices that it had traveled through on its journey. "Who do you know so far north?"

"Nobody, as far as I know," Emily said. She took the letter and opened it cautiously.

"What does it say?" Marta asked impatiently, her eyes alight with interest. Emily scanned it quickly, then read it aloud.

Dear Miss Watson,

Thank you for your letter. I found it most interesting. And before we go any further, because you have been utterly frank with me, I must do the same. I did not place the advertisement in the newspaper myself. My dear, now sadly departed, Uncle Edward placed it on my behalf. He seemed to think it is time I take a wife. I, however, have no such intentions, so most of the letters I received found a fiery end.

However, yours did not. Because I do believe that I can help you – or at least I mean to try.

Firstly, I will need as much information as you can give to me. I know that in your letter you said that you do not know very much, but whatever you can glean will be of use to me.

Firstly, you said you live in Boston, is that correct?

And might I have your date of birth?

And did your mother live in Boston at the time of your conception?

You implied that your father perhaps did not live locally, and was there perhaps at the university? If so, do you know what he was studying?

You said that your mother's friend was at their wedding, can she recall which church it was held at?

Does she recall your mother talking about where his family came from?

The initials on the watch, what are they? Do you know what any of them stand for?

I have a hundred other questions but, for now, the answers to these will give me a number of avenues to start my research.

I am staying with friends in Iron Creek, Minnesota, and will return to Boston on 6th September. I would very much like to meet with you in person, so shall we say I treat you to lunch at Parker's, at one o'clock on the 7th? I do not want to waste a moment.

Yours most eagerly

Richard Ball

It was the letter that Emily had dreamed of receiving but had never expected to come. It had been such a long time since she had written her daring request for help, and finally here was the response. She felt tears pricking at the back of her eyes. She squeezed them tightly, hoping that she might stop them from falling, but it was no use. Marta sat down on the bed beside her and put an arm around her shoulders. "You will finally have the answers you seek. It is as well that the letter arrived on time. He would have been most put out if you had not attended lunch."

"At Parker's," Emily said, shaking her head in disbelief, tears flowing down her cheeks. "Where does he think a girl like me will be able to get something fine enough to wear to such a fancy place?"

"He probably didn't even think about that. Men often don't think of such things," Marta said with a warm smile. "But I am sure that we can make you something in time."

"You are a good friend to me, Marta."

"As you are to me, Em. Now, wipe your eyes and let us go for a walk in town so we may see what fashions the ladies are wearing at the moment."

Emily nodded. She poured cold water from the ewer on the dresser into the bowl and splashed her face with the it. It refreshed her immediately. Marta fetched their shawls, and they made their way outside. As they wondered through the streets, the tenement blocks gave way to fine houses and then to the finest stores where everything anyone could ever need or want could be found. They often enjoyed looking in the windows, where some of the stores created fancy displays of their goods. They knew all too well that they would never own such things, but it didn't stop them from creating stories about the life they would lead if they had those buttoned boots or that feathered hat.

But today, they did not look at the windows. Today they watched the elegant ladies as they got down from their carriages. "Look at the way those ribbons flutter," Marta said as a lady in a wine-red organza gown floated past them as if they weren't even there.

"And look at the goose bumps on her arms," Emily said

with a giggle. "On a chilly day like this, you need something a little warmer, no?"

"A slave to fashion," Marta said. She was feigning disdain, but both women would have given everything they owned to be able to wear such a lovely gown, even for an afternoon.

Half an hour later, they had seen enough gowns to be sure of the kinds of things a young woman should be wearing to lunch at a restaurant like Parker's. They stopped at the fabric shop and bought fabric that Marta was sure she could make look expensive, even though it, thankfully, was not. As it was, the fabric would take most of the money that Emily had saved in the hope she might be able to offer something to Mr. Ball, if he replied to her, to pay for his services. He had not mentioned a fee in his letter, but he would need something, she was sure of that. She would simply have to scrimp and save even more than usual.

While Emily made supper, Marta busily sketched her ideas from all they had seen. She worked with deft strokes of the pencil, creating the elegant lines of the gowns almost effortlessly. Emily couldn't help feeling a little envious. She had never been able to draw anything. Just as Emily was ready to serve their food, Marta jumped up out of her seat at the kitchen table and gave a little whoop. "Em, this is it," she said proudly, holding the paper up to show Emily the design.

Hardly able to catch her breath, Emily stared at the picture. If Marta truly could make something so lovely,

Emily would most certainly not look out of place at Parker's. But with only a few days to do so, and Marta's work at the bakery to do as well as cutting out the pattern and sewing it, Emily couldn't help feeling a little anxious about the entire project.

"I love it," she said eventually. "But is it not too much?"

"No, the ruffles and ribbons are quite the thing, you saw the ladies wearing them, didn't you?"

"I didn't mean that," Emily said. "I meant, is it not too much work for you? You work long hours at the bakery and are always exhausted when you return home. I cannot ask you to do more just so I might have a fancy gown."

"We will both have a fancy gown," Marta reminded her. "Don't think I won't be finding every excuse I can muster to wear this once we're done. Isn't it wonderful that we are the same size?"

Emily laughed. "Yes, I suppose it is. You shall have to go walking in the park every afternoon, so we might get use of it."

"Then it is settled," Marta said firmly. "I shall go to bed immediately after supper. Tomorrow, work will begin."

When Emily returned from the mill over the next three days, Marta had her standing on a box so she could check the way the skirt fell, fix the line of the bodice, and make neat nips and tucks to be sure that the gown would fit perfectly. By the time Thursday evening came around, Marta looked exhausted, but she stayed up all night to sew the ribbons and trim onto the gown and woke Emily before she left to go to the bakery for a final fitting. It was done, and it was perfect. Emily felt like a princess in it.

Emily had been concerned that Mr. Gregor would not let her leave the mill to attend the appointment and that all Marta's hard work would be for nothing. But her employer was a kind man. When she had explained the circumstances to him, he had been happy to let her leave early, so she might get home and changed in time – and he had said that he would not even dock her pay. She had assured him that she would be back as soon as her appointment with Mr. Ball was over, but he had told her not to come back until the morning. It was a relief, but one tinged with anxiety – for with Mr. Gregor being so kind, and after Marta's hard work, she had to go through with the meeting.

The idea of a girl like her attending a place like Parker's made Emily very nervous. She was so scared that she would make a fool of herself, but she had to know who her father was and why he had left her and her mother without any further word. It had become imperative to her. So, as she pulled on the gown and pinned her hair carefully, she tried to remind herself that everything would be worth it if Mr. Ball could find her father.

She didn't have the money for a hansom cab, so she walked very gingerly, holding her skirts up high enough that her ankles were showing, so she would not muddy the hem of the dress. It was a long walk, and her arms were aching terribly by the time she got there. Before entering, she took a moment to breathe, then stood as erect as she could, before trying to sweep gracefully toward the doorway as she'd seen fashionable ladies do. She felt like a fool, and it was much harder than it looked. She almost fell over the hem of her gown as she crossed the threshold of the elegant dining room.

The décor was very masculine, and most of the patrons seemed to be men. There was lots of dark wood paneling on the walls, and the tables and chairs were made of matching wood. Crisp white tablecloths were laid on every table, with gleaming silverware at each setting. Waiters in white coats hurried hither and thither, precariously balanced plates of food in their hands. Yet not one of them dropped a thing. The food smelled and looked better than anything Emily had ever seen. She knew that she must look gauche and out of place, staring at everything, but she couldn't help herself.

Mr. Ball was waiting for her. He stood up as the waiter guided her through the tables. Emily couldn't help thinking that the room had been designed by a man as there was barely enough room for a woman in full skirts to squeeze through without causing an incident. Somehow, she managed not to knock over someone else's water glass, but there were moments when she feared the worst. Mr. Ball smiled warmly at her and offered his hand. She was a little surprised at that. She had not seen gentlemen do that to ladies. It seemed to be something they did among themselves, but she reached out her hand and shook his firmly. He grinned. "You have a firm handshake," he noted. "Many men would be glad of such a grip."

"I work in a mill, Mr. Ball," Emily said. "It is hard work, and some strength is required. Many men of your acquaintance have probably not ever done more than sit at a desk."

He laughed out loud. "You are probably quite right about that."

He moved around the table from his own seat and held the other chair out. Emily glanced around and saw a waiter doing the same for another female diner. She watched as he pushed the chair in a little as she sat, so that the seat met her bottom perfectly. Cautiously, she moved toward the table and began to sit. Within moments, she felt the pressure of the seat against the back of her knees. She almost sighed with relief that she would not end up on the floor. Pulling the chair from under her was the sort of joke that the boys she had grown up with would have thought hilarious. She was glad to know that Mr. Ball was not like them.

CHAPTER 6

September 7, 1889, Boston, Massachusetts

"I am glad my letter reached you in time," Richard said as he took his own seat. "One can never be sure when traveling if you will arrive before any correspondence."

"I have never left Boston, so I cannot say I have any experience of that," Miss Watson replied candidly. "But I did enjoy seeing all the stamps upon the envelope. I used to read a lot when I was younger and had the time, and I loved stories about other places. And I like maps."

She stopped speaking, and he wondered if she thought that perhaps he might not be interested in hearing her talk. Usually, when at a business meeting, he did prefer to keep matters concise, but he already found her fascinating. He wasn't sure if her candor was normal or a reaction to the unusual situation that she found herself in, but he wanted to find out. And to do that, he needed to put her at ease. That would mean he would need to speak plainly, too.

"I love maps, too," he said. "I used to plan journeys all over the world. But then I grew up and realized that such adventures are not for men like me."

"Why not?"

"Because, though to you, I am sure, I may seem well-to-do, I am just a lowly lawyer at the beginning of his career. Which means I do all the work for the partners of the firm, and they take all the credit and the money." He grinned at her, and she gave a nervous laugh. "My father was not a wealthy man. Had he and my mother survived, my upbringing would have been very different. As it was, I was raised by my uncle, who worked his way through the ranks of the army to become a major. We traveled a lot around the country, but there was no time to travel for adventure."

"You have still seen more of the world than me," Miss Watson said, seeming a little more relaxed. "I have been inside a restaurant before."

"You handled it well. I think you missed a couple of water glasses in your perusal." He kept his tone light, so she knew he was teasing.

She blushed. "Was I so obvious?"

"I doubt anyone else was even looking," he said, glancing around at their fellow diners. "Most people are too busy worrying about their own concerns, I find."

"Well, I shall hope you are right."

She paused for a moment, but it was clear to Richard that she wanted to say something else. He waited, as she plucked up the courage to do so, trying to look as kindly as he could to encourage her. "Might I be rude," she said tentatively, "and ask what you were doing in Minnesota? It is such a long way away."

Richard was taken aback for a moment. Most women of his acquaintance would never ask so straightforward a question. They would probably wish to know, just as much as Miss Watson seemed to, but their upbringing to always wait for a man to offer such information would make them hold their questions back. He was slightly surprised to find that he much preferred Miss Watson's directness to their coyness. "You may ask, of course," he said. "My Uncle died a short while ago and he left a number of bequests to his friends and family around the country. He insisted that I deliver them personally. I traveled to New Mexico, South Dakota, Chicago, and up to Minnesota on my whirlwind tour."

"Oh," she said softly, her brow furrowed as if she didn't quite understand how anyone might have friends in so many far-flung places.

"He was an officer in the army for most of his life. He had friends in all the places he served," Richard explained.

"Oh," Miss Watson said more loudly as if this explanation made more sense to her. "I am so sorry for your loss."

"Thank you."

They sat quietly for a moment, both unsure of what to say next. Richard realized that he hadn't taken much notice of Miss Watson as she'd arrived. Oh, he'd paid attention to her reaction to Parker's, but not to her. As she removed her plain straw hat and placed it on the chair beside her, he couldn't help noticing her long, slender neck and the soft wave of her rich, dark hair. He smiled to himself when she fidgeted with her hair, perhaps anxious that the hat had ruined the beautiful way she had pinned it. She was very pretty, with freckles spattered over her nose and cheeks, and the deepest blue eyes that he had ever seen.

And then there was the contradiction of her plain hat and the fashionable cut of her gown, though now they were up close, he could see that it was made from a cheap fabric. She had gone to a lot of trouble not to show him up, of that he was certain. He should have thought about it more before suggesting she meet him here. It was too easy to think that everyone was like him. He would not make the same mistake again.

"Would you like me to order?" he asked her softly, remembering that she had said that she had no experience of being in a restaurant. She nodded, giving him a grateful look. "Do you like roast beef?"

"I think so," she said. "It isn't something we can afford. Occasionally, Mom managed to get some for a stew, but nothing good enough to roast."

"It is my favorite," he said. "And Parker's serves the finest roast dinner in Boston."

"I am happy to trust you," Miss Watson said. She gave him a nervous smile.

When the waiter returned, Richard ordered them roast beef with all the trimmings and a bottle of claret. When Miss Watson protested that she did not drink, he assured her that she need not partake if she did not want to, but that it went particularly well with the beef. Concerned she might not like it, he also ordered some fruit punch, hoping that might be more to her taste.

"So, tell me about your mother," he prompted her. "And your father, what you do know. If you don't mind, I will make notes as we talk." She shrugged, so he took out his notebook and pencil from his jacket pocket. "My aunt always said I should be a writer because I always have a notebook with me, and rather than writing down the things I should, I am more often likely to note down the things that make me smile."

That made her smile properly for the first time since she had arrived. Her eyes lit up, and dimples appeared on her cheeks. Briefly, Jonny and Andy's warnings about finding love via the matrimonials page whether he wanted to or not flashed into his mind. He rubbed his chin, then reached for the napkin in front of him and smoothed it out onto his lap. When Miss Watson copied him, he suddenly realized that she was watching everything that was happening around them. She was so determined not to make a mistake. Surreptitiously, he flicked his hand against one of the shiny knives in his place setting, knocking it to the tiled floor with a clatter. "I am such a clumsy fool," he said as he bent down to pick it up.

"No, you are not. You are a kind man, trying to put me at ease by showing that even when a loud noise occurs, that nobody cares," she said.

"I should have known you would see me do it," he said. "Your eagle eyes haven't missed a thing since we arrived."

"How else is a girl like me to know how to behave?" she asked. "We aren't taught social graces where I grew up."

"Just be yourself," he assured her with a smile. "Your manners cannot be any worse than an English lord I once met at work. The man was a pig. Ate shrimp and turkey legs with his fingers – and slurped his soup."

She giggled. "I don't believe you, but I do thank you."

The waiter appeared with their wine. He poured them both a glass, then disappeared again. Miss Watson began to tell Richard about her mother and everything that Harriet had told her about her father. She took the watch and the letters out of her bag and handed them to him. "I trust you to take care of these," she said solemnly.

"I will guard them with my life," he assured her.

"There is no need for that. I would rather you save yourself from a burning building than run in to save these," she said with a cheeky grin.

"I am relieved to hear that," he said with a dramatic exhalation and a swipe of his hand across his brow. "I do rather like being alive." He also rather liked her, and that hadn't been something he had intended at all.

By the time their meal arrived, Richard had filled a number of pages in his little notebook with what Miss Watson could tell him about her father. The information was sparse, but there were at least two avenues he could look at. The first was the church where the wedding ceremony had taken place; though Mrs. Tolman could not remember the name of it, she had been able to tell him the part of Boston it had been in. Churches kept detailed records of all ceremonies performed, so if the wedding had been performed by a real minister or priest, the record would exist. The second was to check the attendance records at Harvard in the year of Miss Watson's birth for students not from Boston who had left suddenly. It was a start, though it might take a lot of painstaking work, trawling through pages of records.

The meal was, as always, well-cooked and delicious. But Richard got greater satisfaction from watching Miss Watson enjoy her meal than he ever had eating anything himself. She savored every bite, her tastebuds enjoying sensations they had likely never before known. He insisted that she try the chocolate cream pie, a dessert that had been served for the first time on the opening day of the restaurant, back in 1856. Her eyes popped wide open as she enjoyed the two-layered cake filled with buttery pastry cream and covered with rich chocolate icing.

"I think I may have died and gone to heaven." She sighed as she put down her spoon and licked her lips. "How does anyone know how to create such a thing?"

"I do not know, but I am very glad that they do," Richard said. "I know you were nervous about meeting me here, but I do hope that you have enjoyed yourself?"

"Oh, I have. It has been wonderful. But we have not yet discussed your fee, and surely, I should pay something toward this incredible meal?"

"I said I would treat you to lunch, and it has been my pleasure to do so. As to a fee, shall we agree to something a little unorthodox?" She gave him a quizzical look. "Perhaps you can pay me for the result? If I cannot find your father, then you owe me nothing. If I do, you pay me five dollars?"

Her expression when he said the amount told him that even though it was unlikely that such an amount would cover even a quarter of the time and resources needed to find someone, she would struggle to find such a sum. But she did not protest. She simply squared her shoulders and nodded stoically. She was proud. She would not take charity. He knew that. But thankfully, she did not know that he was already charging her far less than such an endeavor required.

But five dollars was a fortune to a girl like Miss Watson, probably more than a week's wages as women were often paid so poorly. Once payments for rent and food were made, she probably had little left at the end of the week. It was an amount that could take her some time to save, but given how little information they had, it would take him some time to locate her father – if he was even able to do so. And in that time, he would find a way to not charge her a penny without hurting her pride.

Upon leaving the restaurant, Richard insisted on seeing her home in a hansom cab. She insisted that she was quite content to walk and needed no companion. It was clear to him that she did not like to be any trouble to anyone, and it made her letter to him even more extraordinary. That she felt strongly enough about finding her father to practically beg a stranger to do something for her seemed out of character. That made him more determined than ever to do what he could to find the mysterious Logan J. W.

But it was past two o'clock, and he had to return to his work. Mr. Grantley had been happy to let him take a more leisurely lunch than usual when he had thought that it might bring the firm a new client, but he would not be so happy when Richard returned without the papers signed and a retainer paid. No doubt, Richard would find his afternoon filled with the most tedious work that the senior partner could foist upon him. And he would do every bit of it without complaint. It would be worth it. Meeting Miss Watson had been a delight.

CHAPTER 7

September 14, 1889, Boston, Massachusetts

The bell rang loudly at the end of the shift. Every woman and child rose from their stations, pulled on their coats and shawls, and made their way off the mill floor, chattering happily, glad that another day was done. Emily glanced back at the silent machines, the scraps of fabric and cotton on the floor, and the piles of cotton fabric that had been woven that day. She couldn't help wishing that her life offered more than this for the rest of her days. She knew she was lucky in many ways. Mr. Gregor was a kinder man than most factory and mill owners and he took care of his workers well, but as a woman, her wages were still lower than men doing the same manner of work, and she worked twelve hours five days a week and six hours on Wednesdays.

It was tedious but dangerous work, and a slip could cost her a finger, perhaps even an entire limb.

As she walked home, Emily wondered if her unhappiness at work was what was driving her to search for her father. She longed for a different life, one with clean air and beautiful views, like she had seen in pictures. She had no idea what she would do in this mythical, lovely place, but she knew it would not be working in a mill. She hummed a little to herself as she let her mind wander, losing herself in her daydream, enjoying the sunshine and blue skies and the freedom to be herself. In this dream, she was loved by a father who wanted her and by a faceless man who cherished her as much as she adored him.

But such fantasies were silly nonsense. Emily had not heard a thing from Mr. Ball since their meeting, and she was beginning to fear that he had perhaps decided that trying to find her father would be too much trouble. She knew well enough that the fee he had stipulated was much lower than it should be. Just because she was poor did not mean that she didn't know that fancy lawyers and their investigations cost large sums of money. But she continued to hold out a modicum of hope that one day she would know her father's name and that he was still alive and would want to meet her.

She had left Parker's feeling that her world was about to change and that she would, at last, have the answers to all her questions. Mr. Ball had been so kind and generous. He had seemed as committed to finding her father as she was. He had also been easy on the eye, with his chiseled features, golden hair, and twinkling blue eyes. She had believed he would be her knight in shining armor, the one to save her from the misery of not knowing. But as the days had passed without word, she had come to think that she would have to save herself.

As she let herself into the house, she called out to Marta. "Are you home?"

"In the parlor," Marta called back.

Emily frowned. They did not have a parlor. The house was too small for anything more than the kitchen and a tiny room where they had a couple of chairs and a fireplace. They must have company – but she could think of nobody who would make Marta call the back room a parlor. She took off her coat and hat and hung them on the peg by the door, then crossed the kitchen to the back room. She pushed aside the curtain that they used instead of a door and was surprised to see Mr. Ball sitting on her chair, sipping tea. He looked as comfortable and at ease as he had at Parker's, as if he experienced such homes every day of the week.

"Good day, Mr. Ball," she said politely.

"Good day to you, Miss Watson," he said, jumping to his feet and nodding his head politely. "Miss Pauling has been kind enough to make me some tea and give me some of her delicious cake. I have been quite spoiled."

"She works in a bakery," Emily said a little foolishly. He must know that. Marta was bound to have told him when she gave him the slice of cake.

Marta stood up and moved to Emily's side. She took her hand. "Mr. Ball has some news for you," she said gently. "I shall leave the two of you to talk alone. I must get our supper ready."

"Thank you, Marta," Emily said, squeezing her friend's hand, not entirely willing to let it go.

"Yes, thank you, Miss Pauling, for looking after me so well," Mr. Ball added enthusiastically. Marta nodded to them both and disappeared behind the curtain. Emily was sure that she would probably listen to every word they said, but it was kind of her to give them the semblance of privacy.

Emily took Marta's seat by the fire. Mr. Ball sat back down in Emily's. He looked tired, with dark circles under his eyes. He had obviously been working very hard. There were lines on his forehead she did not recall seeing before, and his hair was a little disheveled. As if he knew she was looking at it, he ran a hand through his golden locks, trying to smooth them a little.

"I must apologize for my tardiness in coming to see you," he said quietly. "I have been most unusually busy at work this past week and had little time to research your father's identity."

"I understand," Emily said, her heart sinking. She had

suspected something like this, that a man such as Mr. Ball would not find time for her trivial concerns. He had obviously come to tell her that he just did not have the time to pursue her father.

"I have not had much free time, but every moment I have had, I have been sweet-talking clergy at the churches in the district your Mrs. Tolman spoke of. I have ruled out four of the five, as they have no record of a marriage around the dates that Mrs. Tolman gave you. However, I have a meeting at the fifth tomorrow afternoon, and I wondered if, perhaps, you might wish to accompany me?"

It wasn't particularly good news, but it was at least something. Emily could not believe how relieved she felt that Mr. Ball had found time for her despite how busy he had been. She should have trusted him. After all, he had responded to her plea and offered to help for much less money than he should have charged. Her initial instinct had been that he was a good man. She should have trusted herself more. She should have trusted him.

"I would be delighted to accompany you," she said. "Do you really think we might find him there?"

"If he and your mother were indeed married in the district that Mrs. Tolman remembers, then it is the only likely place we might find him," Mr. Ball admitted. "Though I have yet to hear from Harvard, so there may still be hope if we do not find him tomorrow."

"I cannot thank you enough. I had convinced myself that you had decided it was not worthy of your time," she admitted with a rueful smile.

"I feared you might. I intended to write to you to explain almost every day since we parted, and every day, things were so busy that I forgot. I hope you can forgive me."

"Of course. There is nothing to forgive. You have already done so much for me. Would you at least stay for supper? Marta is an excellent cook."

"I should be delighted," Mr. Ball said with a grin. "If dinner is even half as delicious as that apple cake, I shall go home well content."

Emily smiled at him, then ducked behind the curtain to tell Marta. "Did you hear everything?" she asked her friend.

"No, not a word. He speaks very softly, doesn't he?"

"He does."

"And is very handsome," Marta said, raising an eyebrow. "You did not mention that when you came back from your fancy lunch."

"I barely noticed," Emily said as nonchalantly as she could.

"Nonsense. Nobody can ignore a man that handsome," Marta chided.

"Well, even if I did think he was handsome, it does me little good. A gentleman, a lawyer, such as Mr. Ball would not look twice at a mill girl like me, so while he may be pleasing to the eye, it would be foolish to let myself think anything else."

"Well, I'm going to," Marta said with a grin. "He's positively the stuff of dreams – and dreams hurt nobody."

Emily gave her a look of exasperation. Marta was a hopeless romantic. She truly believed that love would win in the end, even though she knew all about Emily's own family history where love had most certainly not conquered all. "You will get yourself into trouble one day," Emily warned her friend.

"No," Marta said happily. "I'm too sensible to ever truly let myself believe that my dreams might come true. But I won't ever stop dreaming them. I have to hope for a better life than this. Don't you?"

"All the time," Emily admitted. "But, as you say, it does no good. I sometimes fear it makes it harder to get up and go to the mill each day, thinking that there might be something better out there."

"If things improve for me, I promise I'll take you with me," Marta said, slipping an arm around Emily's waist.

"I'll take you, too," Emily assured her. "But I should get back to Mr. Ball unless you need my help?"

"Everything is almost ready. I'll call you both when it is."

With a sigh, Emily pulled the curtain back. Mr. Ball jumped to his feet again. "You don't need to get up every time I enter a room," she told him.

"Oh, but I do. A gentleman always rises when a lady enters the room," he said solemnly. "My aunt would be disappointed in me if I did not."

"Your aunt is not here, and Marta and I are not ladies."

"Of course you are," he said. "You might not have been born into wealth, but it doesn't make you any less a lady."

"In your eyes," Emily said pointedly. "Nobody else's."

"Your father must have felt the same way," Mr. Ball said. "If he did not, he would not have wed your mother. Heaven knows, most men would not do so."

"Yet, he let his family take him away from my mom. He may have thought her a lady and respected her, but he did not have the courage to stand up for her. Or for me."

"No, perhaps he did not. But we do not yet know why he felt he had to leave. Perhaps you should not judge him too harshly before we know more?"

His kindness and willingness to learn the truth were endearing. Yet, Emily couldn't help thinking that he was able to be that way because of his upbringing. When a man has everything he needs, all the opportunities in this world open to him, he can give others the benefit of the doubt. She and Mom hadn't been so lucky. They had fought hard for everything they had. She struggled to trust people when so many people in her life had shown her their worst. She envied Mr. Ball because he was still able to seek out the good.

Thankfully, Marta called them through for supper before

she had to respond. Mr. Ball was as appreciative of the thick stew that Marta had prepared as he had been of the roast beef in Parker's. Emily was grateful for that. She would have hated for Marta to feel bad if he had not enjoyed her cooking. She pulled out an apple pie for their dessert, a treat they rarely enjoyed.

"Oh, boy," Mr. Ball exclaimed as he took in the sight of the crisp pastry and smelled a waft of cinnamon as Marta took it from the oven. "I love apple pie."

"I'm afraid there is no cream to go with it, but I hope you like it."

"No cream needed," he said firmly. "Why ruin a work of art with something that dulls the flavor?"

Marta giggled, obviously flattered, Emily kicked her under the table and gave her a warning glare. Mr. Ball was not someone to flirt with. Marta glared back at her, then beamed at Mr. Ball as she cut him a generous slice of pie. "Here," she said a little coyly. "I hope you like it."

When he finally left, Emily turned on Marta. "What were you thinking? Please, don't flirt with him. I don't want him to think less of us. I need him to find my father."

Marta looked immediately chastened. "I'm sorry. I didn't think," she admitted. "I just thought that when you said you weren't interested..." She tailed off, biting at her lip.

"I'm not interested because he is my lawyer. I cannot afford for him to give up the search, though I'm also not entirely sure I can afford for him to continue it, either. But that is a different subject entirely."

"I promise I will not flirt with him ever again, or at least not until he has found your father," Marta said with a cheeky grin. "A girl would be a fool to let a man like that get away if there is even the tiniest chance he might want her, too."

CHAPTER 8

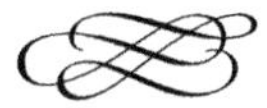

September 15, 1889, Boston, Massachusetts

Richard dressed carefully the next morning. He had two people to impress, after all. Most importantly, he wanted Miss Watson to know that he took her case as seriously as any other he was working on. Secondly, he hoped to make a good impression on Father Michael, who had been a little prickly about showing Richard his parish records. That was why he had asked if Miss Watson would accompany him today; he hoped that when the rather irascible old priest met her, his heart might go out to her.

He chose to walk to the church. Since meeting Miss Watson, he had begun to eschew some of the things he took for granted, such as hansom cabs, as he had realized that they were a luxury for most, far out of reach. It was strange, but he felt much better for it, stronger in many ways. He also rather liked the time it gave him to think, solve problems, and consider what his next steps should be. But he never let himself forget that he was choosing this when many people had few choices about anything and simply did all they could in order to survive.

Miss Watson was waiting at the church door when he arrived. She was dressed in the elegant gown that she had worn to Parker's. The sight made him smile, knowing that she had made an effort, as he had done. She smiled tentatively as he approached her.

"Good morning," he said cheerfully, doffing his top hat as she bobbed him a pretty curtsey.

"Good morning," she echoed. "I think the service will be starting in just a few minutes. We should hurry and take our seats."

"I must confess, I am always just about on time for anything," Richard said, offering her his arm. "I hope you weren't waiting long?"

"No more than fifteen minutes," she said with a smile. "I am always early for everything. I hate to be late."

"Oh dear."

"I shall forgive you, now that I know what to expect," she said lightheartedly.

Richard couldn't help smiling throughout the service as he thought about that brief exchange. He doubted that she had meant anything by it, but her words and tone had been almost flirtatious. And that meant that she liked him, and that gave him a pleasure he had not expected. She was his client. He should have nothing more than a professional manner when with her, yet there was something about her that he just couldn't help liking far more than he should.

He watched as she bowed her head in prayer and as she raised her voice to intone the words of the service. It was clear that Miss Watson attended church regularly, and that her Catholic faith meant a great deal to her. She hung on to every word that Father Michael said during the sermon and seemed genuinely moved by the readings from the Bible. Richard had never much understood blind faith, but it was clear that Miss Watson's faith was not given lightly. She had been tested throughout her life, yet she seemed to find great solace in her faith. He rather wished he felt that way himself.

When the service was over, they made their way to the vestry. Father Michael was folding his ceremonial garments. "It was a lovely service," Miss Watson said, moving toward him. He smiled at her, and Richard knew that he had done the right thing in bringing her. The old man's grouchy expression melted into a warm smile.

"Thank you, my dear," he said, taking her hands in his. "It is a pleasure to preach a sermon to ears that wish to hear God's message. I don't think I have seen you in the church here before, though your face is very familiar to me for some reason."

"No, I live about four miles away from here, though I

believe that my mother used to live in this parish before I was born," Miss Watson said.

"And Mr. Ball here tells me that you think she may have attended church here, or was at least married here?" Father Michael asked as he moved toward an elegantly carved cupboard in the corner of the vestry. He took a key from the ring he had at his waist and turned it in the lock of the door. The hinges creaked a little as he opened it. "I must get some oil," he said with a smile. "I say I will every time I open this, but I always forget."

"Perhaps Mr. Ball can go and find some now?" Miss Watson said, grinning at Richard.

He glared at her but realized that the more they could do to help Father Michael, the more helpful he would be. "I'd be glad to," he said. "If you tell me where to look."

Father Michael chuckled. "There should be some in the janitor's closet. Go through the door there." He pointed at a door at the back of the vestry. "There is a small hallway with three doors. Take the one in front of you. It should be open."

Richard left the two of them alone and fetched the oilcan. When he returned, he found them bent over the parish records for the year that Mrs. Tolman had said Miss Watson's mother had married. "Now, you said your mother's name was Janet?" Father Michael clarified softly. "And your father was Logan, but you don't know his surname?"

"That's right," Miss Watson said, glancing over at

Richard as he oiled the hinges and tried the doors. They opened and closed without a sound. She beamed at him.

"There were only three weddings here that year. I don't think it could have been either of these two, but I do have a Janet who married a Logan," Father Michael said, pointing to the entry.

Richard hurried to join them at the table and looked at the entry. A Janet Mary Watson of Boston had married a Logan John Winston of Philadelphia. He and Miss Watson shared a look of triumph. It could only be them. "Is there an address for his family?" Richard asked eagerly.

"I'm afraid not, but I do have his father's name and both men's professions," Father Michael said, pointing to the last columns of the entry. "He was a student, and his father, Logan John Senior, was a lawyer, like yourself."

"Then we should be able to find him. There will be records of all the cases he ever worked on in the court records in Philadelphia," Richard exclaimed. "Father Michael, I cannot thank you enough for your help."

"I married them," Father Michael said softly, barely even acknowledging that Richard had spoken.

"You did?" Miss Watson asked.

"That's my signature, there," the priest said. "And I remember them. I remember your mother, Miss Watson. I thought there was something familiar about you as soon as I saw you in the congregation."

"You remember her?"

"I do. She was baptized here, too, and received her first communion. I was just a young man then, barely out of seminary. She was kind to me when I made mistakes, even when her friends teased me. She asked me especially to marry her. I can hardly believe that you are here now, looking for your father when they were so very much in love."

"That is what we are trying to find out, Father," Miss Watson said sadly. "But I am glad to know that you believed them to truly be in love."

"Oh, most passionately so," Father Michael assured her. "I don't think I've ever married a couple so devoted to each other. I can only imagine that there must have been a very, very good reason for them to have parted, though I cannot imagine what that might have been."

Having thanked Father Michael for his assistance, and after Richard had put a large donation in the church funds, he and Miss Watson made their way out into the churchyard.

"Well, that was far more successful a visit than I could have ever hoped for," Miss Watson said, her eyes filled with tears. Richard gave her a sad smile. He could understand why what they had just learned might be bittersweet for her.

He handed her his handkerchief, feeling a little awkward. He had no experience comforting upset young ladies. She pressed it to her eyes and gave him a thankful look.

"At least you know that he loved your mother whatever happened next," Richard said tentatively. "And we know his name now. I can give it to the dean at Harvard. That will make your father easier to find. They should have an address for his family, at least."

"I'm not sure if knowing that someone other than Harriet was sure how much they loved each other makes it better or worse," Miss Watson said sadly. "In some ways, it makes his leaving seem even more unforgivable."

"I am still convinced that he must have had his reasons."

"But did he tell my mother them? And if he did, why did she not tell me about him? And why did she not take his name? After all, they were legally married – and until her death, I presume, remained so. It certainly explains why she never seemed interested in finding a husband."

She tucked her arm through his, and they walked slowly through the graveyard. "I'm going to hail a hansom cab, and you are not to argue," he told her firmly. She gave him a wan smile, and for once did not protest. Luckily, a hansom passed by just a few moments later. He helped Miss Watson inside, then got in beside her.

"Do you want me to continue looking?" he asked her as they pulled into her street. "I can understand if you need time to think about things, to decide if you really want to find Mr. Winston or not?"

"We have come this far," she said bravely. "It would be churlish to end the search. Besides, I still have more questions than answers, and that needs to be rectified."

"So, you wish me to continue my inquiries at Harvard?" he asked.

"I do," she said firmly. "I have to know why he left her. And what, if anything, she knew about it."

The carriage came to a halt. Richard opened the door, then jumped down. He let down the steps and offered Miss Watson his hand. She smiled at him. "I can jump down as well as you, you know," she said with a grin.

"I am sure you can. But I was raised a gentleman, and a gentleman always offers a lady his assistance."

She shook her head but took his hand. But he did not let it go once she was out of the carriage, her feet firmly on the cobbled street. He raised it to his lips and pressed a gentle kiss to her pale, cold skin. When he looked up at her, she looked discomfited, but she did not pull away. Richard stood upright and smiled at her. "I have a busy week at work, but I hope I will have time to visit the dean. I will be in touch as soon as I have."

"I finish work at two o'clock on Wednesdays," she told him. "Otherwise, I am not back until seven."

"Noted," he said, nodding. "And dear Miss Pauling, I presume, goes to bed early due to her position in the bakery."

"She does."

"Then I will try to see the dean before Wednesday so I can call on you at a reasonable hour. I would not wish to deprive your friend of her well-earned rest."

"I am sure she would be grateful for your consideration," Miss Watson said, her tone a little sharp.

As he drove away, Richard could not think why her manner toward him changed. There had been moments when he had been sure that something was growing between them, a closeness he had not been looking for. He enjoyed Miss Watson's company. She made him laugh, and she was full of life in a way he had not encountered before. She was proud and brave, and his client. Perhaps she had been annoyed with him because he was getting too familiar. He had to remember that there were boundaries between them. It would not do to get carried away with silly romantic notions about Miss Watson, who had contacted him because she needed his help.

CHAPTER 9

September 18, 1889, Boston, Massachusetts

Marta had gone to visit an old lady from church, who was unwell, and Emily was glad of it. She would normally enjoy her friend's company, but she did not want her friend to distract her lawyer from the task at hand. From what he'd said and the way that he had said it, it was clear that he liked Marta almost as much as Marta liked him. And though she had fought with herself ever since, she had finally accepted that she was jealous. For all her protestations to Marta about not noticing how handsome he was, how kind and funny, she saw all those things and more.

But she had to try to forget all of that now. He would be arriving at three o'clock, according to the note a young lad had delivered to her outside the mill as she'd left for the day. She smiled as she wondered if he would be right on time or a few minutes late. She glanced at the clock on the mantel and tapped her fingers on her arm in time with the second hand, hoping that, for once, he would be early. She was already out of her mind wondering what he had learned from the dean at Harvard.

He banged on the door exuberantly just a few minutes later. Emily jumped up to answer his knock. He beamed at her. "I have his family's address in Philadelphia," he said, clearly delighted with himself.

"You do?"

"I do," he confirmed, showing her a piece of paper. On it, scrawled in an almost illegible hand, was an address that meant nothing to Emily, though it might come to mean everything in the world. "And I have arranged to take a few days of leave so that I can visit, in person. I will be leaving on the four o'clock train today."

"Your employers don't mind you doing that?" Emily asked, aghast. Mr. Gregor was kind and had given her time off to attend her mother's funeral and to move from her house, but even he would object to one of his workers taking a number of days off work. He would fire them rather than keep a place that needed filling. It was yet another symbol of the different worlds that she and Mr. Ball lived in.

"Do you think they still live there?" she asked once he had assured her that he would not lose his position.

"I don't know. It is possible. Most wealthy families, if his is wealthy, tend to have a place that has been in the family for generations. It would take a lot for someone to sell a home like that. Even if they don't live there any longer, the current tenants may know where they moved to."

"Could you not just send a letter or a telegram?" Emily asked, stunned that he would spend so much money to take this trip. The railway tickets alone would be more than five dollars, she was sure.

"I could, but this will be quicker. I can follow up on any other leads I find while I am there. I will, however, send you a telegram every day so you do not need to fret until I return to find out what is happening."

"I think you may have to increase your fee, Mr. Ball."

He rolled his eyes at her. "I must leave, or I shall miss my train. Take care of yourself while I am gone," he said fervently.

"I shall. You must be careful, too."

She waved him off. As his carriage turned the corner, she sighed. It did not feel right that he was going to so much trouble on her behalf. She still did not have even half of his fee saved, and he had already spent more than she was to pay him. He had done that by simply buying them lunch at Parker's. She felt terribly indebted to him, but she could not bear to tell him to stop searching. She still needed to know the answers to her questions. She needed to know that her father was not a bad man, that something more important than her and her mother had called him away.

She was grateful that she had work to do as she waited

for news. Each day, true to his word, Mr. Ball sent her a telegram. His first told Emily that he had arrived safely in Philadelphia. The second, that he had visited the house but nobody had been home. His third said that a neighbor had told him that they were spending some time at their lodge in the country and that Mr. Ball was going to go there before he came back to Boston. His final telegram stated that he had not been received. As she read it, Emily felt her heart sink. They had come so close to finding her father, yet she was still so far away from meeting him, knowing him.

"You cannot let it get you down," Marta said to her as they sat by the fire on Sunday evening. "At least you can always say you tried to find him."

"And found you a beau," Emily said, trying to tease but mostly sounding put out.

"Your Mr. Ball wouldn't look at a girl like me when he's got a girl like you standing right in front of him," Marta said simply. "What wouldn't I do to have a man look at me the way he looks at you?" She pretended to swoon.

"Don't be so silly. He likes you. I know he does," Emily said, shaking her head.

"Oh sure, he likes me in the way it is important to like a girl's best friend, but I can assure you that Mr. Ball only has eyes for you."

"If only that were true." Emily sighed. "And even if it was, I think the situation my poor mom found herself in with a man like Mr. Ball just shows it would never work."

"Things are different now, and Mr. Ball is different from other men of his class," Marta said. "He's much less snooty."

Emily laughed. "True enough, but that doesn't mean that his family isn't all fancy and la-di-da."

"I don't think he's the type to care what his family thinks," Marta said optimistically.

"I don't think you can tell until someone is put in that position," Emily said a little sadly. "And I am unlikely to ever see him again once he returns. We've reached a dead end in our investigations now."

"He's not the type to give up," Marta said simply.

"No, but maybe I am," Emily admitted. "I am tired of jumping at every sound, of lying awake wondering how my father would react if I was ever able to meet him face to face. I cannot do any of it."

Marta moved across the room, perched on the arm of Emily's chair, and put an arm around her shoulders. Emily nestled her head against her friend's warm body and let herself cry. The past months had been as emotional as losing her mother. She felt as though she had lost another parent, even though she had never really had him. Wherever Logan John Winston was, she wished him well, but perhaps it was time to stop searching for him.

An unexpected knock on the door announced another telegram delivery. Emily handed it to Marta, almost unable to bring herself to open it and read whatever it was Mr.

Ball had to say this time. Marta opened it and began to read.

Need to return to Minnesota more quickly than planned. Will visit upon my return, may be some weeks.

Stay well, yours, RB

"Well, I think that answers everything," Emily said sadly. "He's not even coming back to Boston."

"That doesn't mean he doesn't care, just that there is something he has to do for himself," Marta insisted. "Stop feeling sorry for yourself. You were happy before you knew anything about your father. It is time to remember that your mom was a fine parent, the best anyone could ask for, and she was both mother and father to you."

The days passed with no further word from Mr. Ball, and Emily found herself reflecting too often upon their time together. She missed him more than she would have ever thought possible. Just knowing that there might be a note from him or an unexpected visit had brought such pleasure to her life. She was not lonely. She had the Tolmans, Marta, and everyone at church. But her feelings for Mr. Ball had been different, more complicated, and altogether more intense. Without realizing it, she had fallen in love with him – and she only knew that now because her heart was breaking at the thought that she might never see him again.

Poor Marta had the patience of a saint. She was comforting and knew when to back away and give Emily space. She baked special treats daily in the hope they would comfort Emily. But being so distracted at work was proving to be dangerous. On at least four different occasions, Emily had come close to catching her hands in her loom, though she had not done it even once before – not even when she had been learning her trade. Despite that, she couldn't seem to stop herself from thinking about Mr. Ball.

Oh, she had tried to convince herself that it was simply because he was the only person who might be able to bring her father back into her life, but in truth, it was because she could not bear that Mr. Ball was no longer in her life. She missed him. She missed his smile. She missed his optimism and determination that they would find Logan John Winston. Without him, she wouldn't even know her father's name. He had changed her life totally, and she wasn't sure she could go back to a life without him in it, no matter how happy she had thought she was back then.

After another sleepless night, she made her way to the mill. She took off her coat and put on her apron, then made her way to her loom. She checked the threads and the treadle, ensured that her bobbins were full, and started work, sending the shuttles through the threads, back and forth. She felt her body ease into the rhythm. She'd been working there so long that it was almost second nature to her. She hummed to herself as she worked, glad that her mind seemed to be free of thoughts for once.

But a cry behind her disturbed her rare moment of peace among the clanging and clattering of the looms. She stopped working and turned to see one of the older women, Marjorie, gripping a bloodied stump that had once been her hand. Marjorie had taught Emily to weave. She had taught most of the younger women there, in fact. She was the most experienced worker in the mill. Accidents happened in places like this, often. The machines had so many moving parts, and a moment's lapse of concentration could cause permanent damage. As Marjorie had done now. Emily hurried her off the floor and into the small room where the most basic of medical supplies were kept. Marjorie needed a surgeon, but Emily doubted if she had the funds to pay for one.

Mr. Gregor appeared in the doorway. "Marjorie, oh what have you done?" he cried, falling to his knees before her. He took the bandages from Emily and took over from her. "Emily, go and see Dr. Galen. His office is just opposite. He'll know of the best surgeon to take Marjorie to."

Emily nodded. As she ran across the street, she could only feel a peculiar sense of relief. In the past days, she could have been where Marjorie was now. She had not been paying attention. It was an important reminder that she needed to forget Mr. Ball, forget about finding her father, and simply get on with her life.

Dr. Galen came straight away, and he and his assistant took Marjorie away to a surgeon friend. Mr. Gregor looked spent. "Let no expense be spared," he called loudly to them. "Marjorie, don't you worry about a thing. I shall pay for it all." He sank down on the seat Marjorie had just left. "She's been with me from the beginning," he said shaking, his head in disbelief. "She's the very heart and soul of this place."

"She is, Sir," Emily said sadly. "And I will let the girls know that you're looking after her. They'll be glad to know that."

"I must go to her," he said, suddenly decisive. "The machines are not to be turned back on today. I shall call in an engineer to see if there is more we can do to protect you all, but I won't let any of you work until then."

"Wonderful as all that sounds, Mr. Gregor, none of us can afford to live if we aren't getting paid our daily rate," Emily said simply.

He paused for a moment. He had probably never been spoken to that way by one of the mill floor girls, and it was clear to him that he had not even considered the financial implications of his actions. Wealthy men didn't have to. When you're at the bottom of the ladder though, it's the first thought to cross your mind. "None of you will be docked even a moment's pay, I assure you," he said. "And I promise I will take care of Marjorie financially, too."

"Thank you, Sir. I am sure her family will be glad to know that."

"I do hope they won't blame me," Mr. Gregor said, suddenly cautious. "Would you go in my stead to see them and tell them?"

Emily thought about what she would prefer if she was in the shoes of Marjorie's family. She wouldn't want to hear such a thing from one of Marjorie's fellow workers. They would need confirmation that they would not lose their wages or have to pay for their loved one's care from the man capable of doing so. "No, Sir. I think it would be better if it comes from you," she said softly.

CHAPTER 10

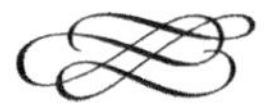

September 23, 1889, Iron Creek, Minnesota

It was good to be back at Pinewood Lodge, along with his aunt, whom he had invited to join him. Richard was surprised to realize just how much he had missed the town of Iron Creek, and especially the people within it. He had only been there for a short visit the last time, but it had been long enough for him to know that it was the kind of place he could make his home when he was ready to settle down. He sat at the desk in the parlor, looking out over the mountains, and tried to write a letter to Miss Watson. He had tried to do so many times since he had received the telegram from Jonny telling him that Andy and Amy had given birth to a healthy baby girl and that they wished him to stand as godfather to their second born, in honor of his uncle.

Of course, such an offer was not one he could pass up lightly, but he feared that he may well have pushed the limits of the amount of leave that the firm would permit him to have. It was strange, but he didn't care. Since his uncle had passed away, Richard had come to believe that it was important to live life fully – and he was not doing that festering away as little more than a clerk at Grantley, Bedford, and Chesterton. And the pay was terrible. The only reason he was able to live in comfort at all was because of the annual stipend that Uncle Edward had left him.

"Richard, dear, I do not know how many times I will say it, but isn't that bathroom a marvel?" Aunt Mary said as she came into the parlor, having enjoyed yet another hot bath in the large tub. "I cannot tell you how glad I am that you convinced me to come with you. A stay in the mountains has been positively therapeutic for me."

"I am so glad you like it here," Richard said, smiling warmly at her. "I hoped you would. It reminded me of that place you loved in South Dakota. I don't remember its name."

"Nor do I, but I think I know where you mean. I think Iron Creek is even lovelier, even though it is already so cold here."

"I'm glad Jonny warned us to pack warm clothes and thick coats."

Aunt Mary sank down onto the couch. "I could stay here forever," she said wistfully.

"I must confess, I was thinking along those lines before you emerged from your bath," Richard admitted. "I love it here. I love the people, and I think I could be of use here. People have real legal problems in places like this."

"Then why don't you move here?" Aunt Mary asked. "There's nothing to keep you in Boston."

"There's you," he pointed out. He didn't mention Miss Watson. She wasn't his to miss, though he longed to see her terribly.

"I'd gladly move here. Find another excuse," she teased. "Are you ever going to tell me about the young lady you've met?"

"There's no young lady," Richard protested, but his aunt knew him too well.

"There most certainly is a young lady," she said. "I am not a fool. You've been different ever since you took on trying to find that poor child's father."

"And I am still no closer to doing that," he admitted. "I hate that I failed her."

"You aren't dead yet, and neither is she. You have time. You can keep looking. Wear down those people you went to visit. Nobody can resist you forever. You are just too charming, just like your dear uncle was."

Richard smiled at her, and they both made their way into their separate bed chambers. Aunt Mary had laid a clean shirt and his best suit on the bed, prior to the imminent christening service. He smiled, remembering that she had always done the same for Uncle Edward.

Jonny, his wife Cassie, and their young son Danny were waiting in the hotel foyer for them a few minutes later. It was clear that Cassie would soon be giving birth to another child herself. "Congratulations," Richard said, pressing a brotherly kiss on her cheek.

"Jonny is sure it will be another boy, but I am praying for a girl. I feel terribly outnumbered sometimes," she said, giving her husband and son an indulgent look.

"It would be good company for Andy and Amy's little one, too, as Danny is for Edward."

"I know that my husband would have been very honored to know that one of you named their son for him," Aunt Mary said with a sad smile. "He was very fond of you both."

"As we were of him. Tough but fair," Jonny said.

They clambered into the carriage outside, and Jonny drove them into Iron Creek. The church was already filling with people when they arrived. Everyone greeted them with a wave and a smile. Andy was in his wheeled chair with Edward perched on his lap, and Amy was standing at his side, holding baby Evie.

"I still cannot believe you were able to get here," Andy said as Richard reached them. The two men shook hands firmly, then Richard greeted Amy with a kiss.

"May I?" he asked, holding his arms out to his goddaughter.

"Of course," she said, handing over Evie without hesitation. "She's a little grizzly today."

"Not at all, are you my little darling," Richard crooned to the baby, who looked up at him with her big blue eyes and immediately calmed down.

"She's mesmerized," Amy marveled.

"So is he," Aunt Mary said with a chuckle. "I don't think it will be long before I am made a great aunt, do you?" Richard glared at her, but everyone else laughed.

Father Paul conducted the service with reverence and kindness and gave a touching sermon. Everything went perfectly, right up until the moment when he blessed Evie with the holy water in the font. A heart-wrenching cry rang out throughout the church as she made it known that she most certainly did not like being made wet. Richard took her from the priest and held her tightly against his chest. She stopped crying almost immediately, and knowing she was safe in his warm, strong arms, she soon stopped grizzling again and fell fast asleep.

Jonny and Andy both made a point of introducing Richard and Aunt Mary to the people he had not met on his last visit. Aunt Mary was soon chattering with Nelly Graham and Mrs. Cable as if the three had been lifelong friends. Knowing she was settled, Richard felt free to mingle. Mayor Winston was one of the people he wished to speak with. If he and Aunt Mary really did intend to move there, he would need the mayor's approval.

"Mr. Ball, I believe," the mayor said, holding out a hand in greeting as Richard approached him.

"Richard, please," he said as he took the man's hand and shook it firmly. It reminded him for a moment of the day he had shaken Miss Watson's hand, they shared an unusually similar grip. "I am glad I have been able to see you. I believe you were away on my last visit."

"Indeed, I had some legal matters to take care of on behalf of the town, and the closest lawyer is in Grand Marais. I have tried and tried to attract one here, but we seem to get everything but." He paused and gave Richard a thoughtful look. "I don't suppose I could convince you to move here, could I? Jonny tells me you're a lawyer."

"I believe you could," Richard admitted. "I fell in love with Iron Creek last time I came, and must confess that I like it even more on my return."

"Then, you must come to my office tomorrow. We can talk it all over, make plans, and get you here as soon as you are able," Mayor Winston said eagerly.

"I would be delighted," Richard said. "Around ten o'clock?"

In the morning, feeling a little weary after the festivities the night before, Richard took a horse from the stables and made his way back to Iron Creek. The mayor's house was the finest in town, right in the middle of Main Street. Richard hitched Bemised to the fence and let himself in through the neat, white gate. The door was open before he'd even made it to the steps up to the porch.

Mayor Winston smiled down at him. "Happy to see you," he boomed.

"And you," Richard said, shaking the mayor's hand. "I can hardly believe my luck that the town has no lawyer, given what everyone has told me about its rapid growth."

"Oh, we did have one, but it's been a long while since Willie Graham passed away." Mayor Winston said. He reached for a set of keys from the hallway table and put his coat on.

"Would that be Mrs. Graham's husband?"

"Yes. He's much missed, by her and all of us in town. Fine lawyer, even finer man."

"So, I have large boots to fill," Richard said as Mayor Winston indicated he should go back down the steps and out onto the street.

"You do, but there's many in town who wouldn't even remember the man, though that is their loss. Now, let us go and see his old offices."

They walked down Main Street and stopped outside a large, glass-fronted shop. "You being interested in coming here, and our need, well, there's those around might say that is fate," Mayor Winston said. He unlocked the door and ushered Richard inside.

"I don't believe in fate, or at least I didn't," Richard said with a smile as he looked around the slightly musty-smelling space. "I think men work hard to find their own way. It would be a rather dismal life, would it not, if man had no agency over his own destiny?"

"Call it fate, call it destiny, whatever it is, it has been most fortuitous for Iron Creek that you were brought here," Mayor Winston said happily as he led Richard to a wood-paneled office in the back of the building. An oak desk dominated the space, and on it was a small pile of papers. "Now, for the formalities – if you are truly sure that you wish to join us?"

"Oh, I am sure," Richard said fervently. "I can think of nowhere better to live, for myself and for my aunt. She loves it here as much as I do."

"You will need to notify the local magistrate and the courts in Minneapolis," Mayor Winston said, handing Richard a slip of paper with two names and addresses upon it. "You don't need to formally apply to practice law here, though I believe there are intentions to create a register of licensed attorneys."

"An excellent way to protect people from unscrupulous, uneducated lawyers," Richard said. "There are far too many who just put a sign up on the door and take their clients for every penny."

"Given you are a Harvard man, I assume that you would not be so dishonest," Mayor Winston said. "At least in my day, there was an expectation that alumnae were of the highest moral caliber."

"You went to Harvard?" Richard said. "Well, it can be a small world, can it not?"

"I did. History department. Changed me in every way," Mayor Winston said thoughtfully. "The very best years of my life."

For a moment, Mayor Winston seemed lost in his memories. Richard didn't know what to say. The mayor looked so melancholy, all of a sudden. But within moments, the older man shook his head and gave Richard an apologetic look, then carried on speaking as if nothing had happened. "I bought this place from Nelly after Willie passed away. It is a fine location that I assumed would soon be filled by another lawyer."

"It is a fine office. With a lick of paint and some new furniture, it will suit me perfectly," Richard agreed.

"I have papers here. You can choose which suits you best." He held up the first one. "This is a deed of sale. You can buy the building. There are some nice rooms above the offices, which would make a fine home for you and your aunt." He put the paper down and held up the second one. "Or you can rent it from me. I'll not charge its full worth, at least not for six months, to give you time to be sure you're going to stay. If you choose to stay, the offer of sale will remain open to you at any time."

"I think it would be wise to take your offer to rent for the first few months at least," Richard said. "And I think that my aunt would prefer to live up the mountain a little rather than in town. She's had enough of the hustle and bustle."

"I can ask around and see if anyone has anything suitable to rent," Mayor Winston said. He handed Richard the rental agreement to read through before he signed it. "I think we can arrange something in time for when you move here. I presume you will need to return to Boston to arrange your affairs there?"

"Yes. I think a month or two would be sufficient for us to deal with everything in Boston," Richard said.

They stood quietly for a moment while Richard read through the contract. After he had read a few paragraphs, he looked up. "Do you have a pen?" Mayor Winston rummaged in the desk and found a pen and a bottle of ink and handed them to Richard, who struck through a number of lines, added words in places, and handed the agreement back to Mayor Winston, who grinned.

"A fine lawyer indeed," he said, noting the changes Richard had made.

"I do not need the rooms, so do feel free to rent them out," Richard said. "I will not pay for space I have no use for."

"Agreed. Now, do you want me to get this written out again with your changes, or are you happy for us to sign it as it is?"

"I think it would be best if it were written out cleanly," Richard said. "I do not want to start my practice here in Iron Creek with a shoddy contract." The two men laughed.

CHAPTER 11

September 25, 1889, Iron Creek, Minnesota

In their final days before they went back to Boston, Richard and Aunt Mary spent most of their time exploring. They took walks down by the creek and, after a quick driving lesson from Jonny, took the gig out so they could explore further afield. Aunt Mary seemed utterly enamored with everything about Iron Creek, from the gently sloping mountains to the incredible variety of birds and wildlife that they encountered on their travels.

On their final drive, they came across an almost derelict ranch house, not far from the Hardings' place. "Oh, what a lovely place that must have been to live in." Aunt Mary sighed as she admired the view from the rather dilapidated porch.

"Be careful, there's more hole in those boards than there

is board," Richard warned her, as he peeked inside the broken windows.

"Can we go inside?" Aunt Mary asked eagerly.

"I doubt it's safe," Richard said. He tried the front door, and it opened with a loud creak. He peered into the darkness, then remembered that there was a lamp on the gig, so he fetched it and lit the candle inside the glass and iron cage. "Let me go first. If anyone is going to fall through this rotten floor, it should be me."

Aunt Mary chuckled. "But I'd be no use in trying to get you out, little old woman like me, great big lumbering fellow like you." Richard gave her a stern look. She had always been the adventurous type. Married to a military man, she had always had to be. It took a lot of courage to set up home in the dangerous places she had found herself in, following Uncle Edward from post to post.

Cautiously, he moved inside the house, holding the lantern above his head to light their way. Aunt Mary followed him closely. The large hallway contained a very grand staircase that curved up and round, leading to a wide landing. It must have looked stunning in its heyday, with its carved oak spindles and smooth treads. Now, most of those beautiful spindles and treads were broken or missing. To the left was a large spacious room that may have been a parlor. A lonely piano stood in one corner. To the right of the hallway was a smaller room with wood-paneled walls and shelves. A few moldy books still lay upon them.

But the finest room by far was the spacious kitchen. The cast iron range sat proudly at one end, filling the entire wall. There was a large sink in front of the window, so whoever was washing the dishes could enjoy a view of what had once been a lovely kitchen garden. Now, that was overgrown, a tangle of weeds and perennials that was impossible to see through. A large kitchen table was in the very center of the room, and some old copper pots hung from the wall. "Oh, I would love to cook in here," Aunt Mary said with a sigh. "If only we could live here."

"Well, I see no reason why we can't," Richard said with a grin, remembering the conversation he'd had with Jonny about how talented the town carpenter was. "Clearly, nobody wants this place. We can find out who owns it, buy it, restore it to its former glory, and live here happily until the end of our days."

"Oh, I cannot tell you how much I would like that. Raising my grandnieces and nephews here would be such a joy."

"How many am I to provide you with?" Richard said, chuckling at how quickly her mind had seen children playing here. He had to admit, it would be a wonderful home to raise children in. He, too, could picture them out on the porch, playing games or reading books together. "I will speak with Mayor Winston about it when I go and sign the rental papers this afternoon. He must know whose place this was."

They made their way back outside and took a couple of

deep breaths of the clean, fresh air. Richard blew out the candle and attached the lantern to the gig before checking his pocket watch. "Goodness," he said. "If I do not make haste, I shall be late. We have spent more time here than I thought. You will have to come with me to see Mayor Winston, Aunt. I don't have time to take you back to the hotel."

"I do not mind. I can go to the bakery and get us some of those lovely pastries they sell while you do your business."

It never ceased to amaze him how unflappable his aunt was. Nothing ever seemed to surprise her or worry her. She was a wonder, and he never stopped feeling lucky that she and Uncle Edward had taken him in as a boy. They had given him love and encouragement and the courage to be himself, despite all the changes of school and town that he had experienced because of their rather nomadic life.

They arrived at Mayor Winston's house five minutes late for his appointment. Aunt Mary couldn't stop laughing as Richard muttered under his breath about what a fool he was and how he hated to make a bad impression. "If you do not wish to be late, you need to remember to be early," she pointed out. "You have always been so easily distracted, and you have no sense of time. I envy it sometimes."

"I do not," Richard said as he secured the lead rein, thinking for a moment about Miss Watson who, like his aunt, was never late for anything. They were both much more fastidious about time than he could ever be. "Now, be sure to buy plenty of pastries. We shall be celebrating the purchase of our new home and my new office when I return."

She smiled and watched him bound up Mayor Winston's path before turning to go to the bakery. Richard glanced back and waved as he reached the top step, then rapped on the door. A young woman opened it and showed him into the mayor's office. The house was as impressive inside as it was imposing outside. It seemed a little ostentatious to Richard, and he had met many men who would suit such a house, however he had not got the impression that Mayor Winston was the sort of man who cared much for such shows of wealth or power.

Moments after he had been left alone in the office, Mayor Winston appeared. "Good day to you, Richard," he boomed. "I have had the contract written out, and I am eager to get it signed."

"I am, too, Mayor Winston," Richard said. "And I am most sorry for being tardy."

"Oh, no matter. I am always here. Always so much to do, making the town funds stretch as far as I can." He smiled. "You'll find that small-town life is not so wedded to the clock as it is in Boston."

"I have noticed that, and I am glad of it. I have never been the most punctual of men," Richard said with a wry smile.

Mayor Winston chuckled. "I would imagine that has made things somewhat difficult for you there. My recollection of the place was that everyone was always in a terrible hurry."

"It has not changed."

"Nor should it. There is a place for cities like Boston and New York, where men of ambition who aspire to wealth can congregate. They cause nothing but mayhem when they settle anywhere else, I find."

"Would it be rude of me to ask where you grew up?" Richard asked. "You do not seem to have any hint of the accent I hear around here. It is closer to Boston, but you talk as if you went to Boston rather than were raised there."

"You are right, I am Pennsylvania-born and raised," Mayor Winston said. "But I wasn't keen on living there either. When my father died, I took my chance to break free, and when an old Harvard friend suggested moving to Minnesota because there were towns in need of men who could find their way around a file or two, I thought why not? I had nothing that mattered to me in Philadelphia."

"Goodness, that was brave," Richard said, surprised that a man like the mayor had made such a reckless move. The more he learned about the man, the more a tiny kernel of an idea was forming in Richard's mind. He didn't dare think it. He couldn't possibly have gotten so lucky as to chance upon the one man he needed to find more than anyone in the world. Could he?

Mayor Winston was still reminiscing. "I clerked for Willie Graham, dear Nelly's husband, when I first arrived here. Learned a lot and began to do odd bits for lots of people in town. When the town grew big enough to need an administration, I was honored when they voted me mayor, and have done ever since."

"You must be doing a fine job," Richard said, his thoughts racing.

"I hope so. I know many would say I am a little too tight with the purse strings, but it is necessary to be prudent in order for things to run smoothly."

"I quite agree." Richard paused for a moment. He wanted to bombard Mayor Winston with questions, but he had nothing more than conjecture to work from at that moment. He knew he had to wait and be patient until he could be sure. It was not good form to go around accusing men of abandoning their wives and daughters when you weren't even sure if you had the right man. And he did not want to put his own future position in the town in jeopardy. He decided it was best to stick to the matters he had come to discuss.

"Given your position," he said, "I am hoping that you might be able to assist me with something. I would be grateful for your advice."

"Tell me," Mayor Winston said, looking intrigued. "If there is anything I can do to help, I will be glad to."

"There is a house on the track up to the Hardings' place. My aunt and I saw it while out driving this morning."

"The old Bailey homestead," Mayor Winston said,

recognizing the place immediately. "My friend, the one who convinced me to come here, well, it was his place. He was a terrible rancher, and he up and left having lost every penny he'd ever had. Lives in Grand Marais and works in a bank now."

"Do you think he would sell us the house?"

"I know he would. He's hoped to get rid of the place for almost twenty years," Mayor Winston said. "And given the state of it, there's not been much interest despite its setting. Garrett Harding bought most of the land just a year or so ago, as his ranch expanded. There's not much more than the pasture out the front and the garden out the back."

"I don't want too much land. I don't have the time to take care of it – or at least I hope I won't," Richard said with a nervous chuckle.

"You will be busy from the moment you open your doors, I can guarantee it. I will give all of the town's legal business to you, which will give the rest of the town confidence in you. I do not doubt you will be very successful here."

"Thank you. Will you approach him on my behalf? I would be glad to know that the sale is in progress before we leave for Boston."

"I will send him a telegram the moment we finish our business here."

"And perhaps I might rent the rooms, after all, while the renovations are undertaken? I cannot help thinking it might take some time to make the place habitable," Richard said with a smile.

"Of course," Mayor Winston said. "Shall we draw up a contract for that separately? It would save us having this one rewritten."

"Hand me paper and a pen," Richard said, laughing. Within moments, a short contract for the rooms had been drawn up and he had put it in front of Mayor Winston to sign. "I can hardly believe that just a few days ago, I was a Boston lawyer, and now I have drawn up my first contract in Iron Creek."

Richard watched Mayor Winston sign the document with a flourish and print his name below. He bent over the page to sign himself and looked more closely at the mayor's tiny writing.

Logan John Winston

He gasped and reread it, unable to believe what he was seeing. There had been so many hints, so many clues, but he hadn't wanted to make any accusations until he was sure. Now he was. "Mayor Winston, did you know a woman named Janet Watson?"

The mayor's eyes opened wide, and his mouth dropped open. "However did you know?"

CHAPTER 12

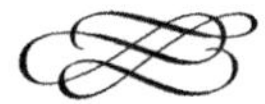

October 15, 1889, Boston Massachusetts

It was dark as Emily left the mill. The nights were drawing in, and her shawl wasn't really warm enough to keep out the chill. She walked briskly to Marjorie's house. Emily visited her as often as she could after her tragic accident at the mill. Little Hal, Marjorie's grandson, opened the door and smiled when he saw her. "Did you bring anything from Marta today?" he asked eagerly.

"I'm afraid not, Hal. But she did say that she would try to get you all a treat for tomorrow." The little boy's face fell. "Now, how is your gran? Have you been taking good care of her?"

Hal nodded. "She's much better today. She helped Mom a little in the kitchen."

"I'm glad to hear that," Emily said.

"Come on through, Emily," Marjorie called from the kitchen. "I wasn't expecting you today."

Hal took her hand and dragged her through to the warm and cozy kitchen. Kathy, Marjorie's daughter, was standing at the stove. Her husband, Mark, was warming his stockinged feet in a chair beside her. Hal took a seat at the table and began playing a game with his sister. Emily took the stool by Marjorie's armchair by the fire. "How are you?" she asked.

"Much better now. I'm getting used to doing things with one hand, and Mr. Gregor has sent me a tutor to teach me how to improve my writing and do sums so's I can work in the offices on my return. Says he'll make a bookkeeper of me yet."

"I am so glad he is doing all he can to make sure you can still work."

"We are lucky. He's a good man. You hear all the stories about girls out on the street when they can't work."

"We're lost without you on the floor," Emily admitted. "It's not the same. Nobody wants to step up and take charge. They're all afraid they'll fall flat on their noses."

"You should," Marjorie said simply. "You're the best worker there, and you're cleverer than any of them."

"Oh, I'm not ready for that," Emily said shyly. "I could never tell women older than me their business."

"You could, and they'd listen, too. Everyone there knows I had you in mind to take over from me when I was gone –

though you're sharp enough that you could do so much better."

"If only people would look at a girl's skills and not her upbringing, that would be easier."

"True enough. But you shouldn't give up trying," Marjorie said. "The mill was a good job for a girl in my day, but there's better things for a clever girl like you. You could be in Service, or even work in one of those fancy department stores that are springing up in the city now."

"I'm not patient enough with people for that," Emily chuckled. "I'm happy at my loom for now."

"But you have dreams, I hope?"

"Of course I have dreams," Emily said with a smile, thinking momentarily about Mr. Ball and his slightly lop-sided smile.

"Ah, there's a boy," Marjorie said perceptively. "And does he look like that when he thinks of you, I wonder?"

"Oh, I very much doubt it," Emily said sadly. "He's a lawyer. Too fancy for the likes of me."

"No such thing as too fancy if you care for one another," Kathy said with a grin. "Mark's sister married a judge, and you're definitely fancier than her."

Mark guffawed. "Ain't that the truth," he agreed.

"And you're very pretty," Hal piped up. "But I want you to wait for me to grow up so I can marry you."

"That is a very kind offer, Hal. I shall keep it in mind," Emily said solemnly. The boy beamed. "But I should get back. I don't like to disturb Marta too much in the evenings. I just wanted to know how you are."

"I'll be back at work within a fortnight, I hope," Marjorie assured her. "I can't wait to get back. I'm bored silly with so little to do."

Emily walked home quickly. It was only two blocks away, but it always felt more dangerous walking around alone in the dark. There weren't too many gas lamps in this part of town, and all manner of folk lurked in the dark corners at night. She was about to let herself into the house when a dark shadow emerged from the alleyway to the side of the house. Emily almost screamed until she saw the profile of the man in the light from the window.

"Mr. Ball, whatever are you doing here at this time of night?" she asked. She opened the door and ushered him inside.

"I came to see you," he said as if it were the most obvious thing in the world. "I've been waiting for you. As there were no lights, I presumed Miss Pauling must have gone to bed. I didn't want to wake her."

"But why?" Emily shook her head. "Not why is Marta in bed, but why are you here? I thought we had established that we had reached a dead end and that without a miracle we would be unlikely to learn anything more about who my father might be?"

He beamed. "Because a miracle did happen."

She stared at him. "A miracle happened?" she echoed. "I don't understand."

"I've met your father. Of course, I didn't realize he was your father to start, but he is definitely your father."

"You're babbling," she said, feeling both bemused and amused by his exuberant announcement. "Sit down, let me make us some hot tea, and you can tell me all about it. Slowly."

A light tread on the floor above them made Emily sigh. "We've woken Marta. Be quiet, the poor woman has to be up before the dawn."

"I'm sorry, I forgot. I came here straight from the train. I couldn't wait another minute to tell you. I thought of sending a telegram, but that seemed too impersonal. I had to be here, to tell you in person. It was the most peculiar thing."

"I'm sure. Now, can you please slow down and start at the beginning?"

He watched her fill a kettle with water and place it on the stove.

"I'm afraid we have no sugar," she said apologetically. "But there may be a slice of cake in the cupboard." She lifted the lid of a pot on the stove, stirred it, and sniffed deeply. "Or you can have some of this chicken soup."

"Some soup would be nice," Mr. Ball said. "It is rather cold out tonight."

"Soup it is." Emily fetched some bowls and spoons and

thanked Marta silently for having somehow managed to afford a chicken. Most of their meals weren't suitable to put in front of a man like Mr. Ball. They could rarely manage to afford meat or fish. Thankfully, Marta was a genius in the kitchen and was able to make incredible food from almost nothing.

She dished up the rich, thick soup and placed a bowl in front of Mr. Ball, then another at her own seat at the kitchen table. She poured the now boiling water into the teapot and left it to steep as they ate their meal. "So, tell me what happened," she prompted Mr. Ball as he ate his soup without slurping a single drop.

"I was invited to return to Iron Creek, the place I told you about when I had to deliver all those bequests?"

She nodded. "I remember. You liked it there."

"I did, a lot," he said. "The men I met there were old colleagues of my uncle, and they very kindly invited me to act as godfather for one of their children. I'm sorry I did not have time to come and see you before I went, but I stopped in Boston barely long enough to fetch my aunt."

"You did not need to visit me," Emily said simply, though she had been hurt that he had not even written to her after that hurried telegram from Philadelphia. "You had done all I asked of you and more, and I still have not paid your fee." She got up from the table and went to the mantle in the tiny room at the back of the house. A small box held all her savings. She picked it up and took it into the kitchen. "I will pay you the rest as soon as I can, a little each week."

He looked at the pile of coins in the box. There must have been at least three dollars, possibly a little more, in there. He closed the lid and pushed it away from him. "The deal was that I should find your father," he said softly.

"And from what you have said, you did," Emily said bluntly.

"Not because of my investigation," he said firmly. "I will not accept a fee for finding someone purely by accident."

Emily frowned but could think of no reply. She pushed the box back toward him, but he left it on the table and leaned back in his chair.

"As I was saying," he said gently. "I traveled to Iron Creek to act as godfather to the most beautiful baby girl. While I was there, I got talking to the mayor of the town. He's been there for many years and has been mayor for most of them. He is a well-respected and well-liked man, though many might say he holds the town's finances too close."

"He is miserly?"

"Not at all. More prudent," Mr. Ball said with a smile. "I found him to be generous and kind in my dealings with him, and a little sad."

"Sad?"

"Yes, but I shall get to that. Well, he asked me jokingly if I would like to stay in Iron Creek and become a small-town attorney. Frankly, I couldn't have said yes faster."

"You're leaving Boston?" Emily said, feeling her heart break just at the thought of it.

"I am," he said, his expression suddenly changing. It looked almost as though he now regretted his decision, but he forced a smile. She could tell it was forced because his eyes weren't twinkling like they normally did. "Aunt Mary and I will pack up the house here and get our affairs in order. We hope to move there as soon as possible."

"Goodness," Emily said. "Is such a move not a little rash? You've barely visited the town for more than a few weeks at a time and know barely anybody there. Will you not miss Boston? It all seems so sudden."

"I shall miss some people I have met here," Mr. Ball said, looking into her face as if he was trying to convince them both that everything would be alright. "But you forget, I am used to moving around. I have been in Boston longer than anywhere, I think."

Emily wanted to beg him to stay. Every day of his absence had been hard for her. She had not ever expected to come to care for anyone the way that she cared for him. She knew that her feelings could never be reciprocated, but she wanted to tell him. She wanted him to acknowledge there was something between them, that it wasn't just her feeling this way. But she could not. She did not have the right to ask him to stay. He was her lawyer. Nothing more.

"Sorry, you were telling me the story," she said.

"Yes, well, I went to see him in his office the next day, and he offered me the use of an office building and the rooms above it. We looked at the paperwork and it needed a few changes, so we agreed to meet again later in the week when we would sign the documents and make it official."

"And possibly gave you time to think about the decision you were making?"

"Yes, that, too. Aunt Mary and me, well we went all over the area. On one of our trips, we found an old, rundown house. It was in the perfect setting, but it turned out not to have been lived in for almost twenty years. It needs a lot of work, but I can't think of a better place in all the world to live – and neither could Aunt Mary."

"I am happy for you both," Emily said sadly. "But about my father? Is he the owner of the old house?"

Mr. Ball grinned. "All in good time," he teased. But Emily wasn't in the mood to be teased. She frowned at him. He seemed to get the message.

"Well, I spoke of the house to the mayor, and we agreed to sign the contracts for the law offices. When we went to sign the papers and, well, he signed them Logan John Winston."

"My father's name."

"Yes. I asked him if he knew your mother. There had been so many clues. He shakes hands like you, went to Harvard at around the right time, he came from Philadelphia. But I wasn't certain until that moment."

"And did he say why he left us?" she asked coolly. She wasn't sure how she should feel about the news. She had always thought she would be glad to finally know her father and perhaps be angry with him. But this peculiar nothingness was not something she had considered at all.

"No, he would not tell me. And I don't blame him for that. I am after all a stranger to him. But he said he would tell you if you will visit him in Iron Creek."

CHAPTER 13

October 20, 1889, On the Train

It felt most peculiar to Emily to be traveling so fast, to see the world passing by her window. She was excited but afraid. She glanced across the carriage to where Mr. Ball lounged comfortably, taking a nap. It was all so very normal for him. He did not see the wonder of the vast steam locomotive or care that they had passed through the city and out into the countryside in no time at all. He seemed unconcerned that the bed in her sleeping compartment was more comfortable than the one in her home, and even less worried that porters and waiters kept asking if there was anything they could do for them. It would take a lifetime for her to get used to that.

As the trees and fields passed by the window, she thought about everything that had happened in the past five days. It had taken Mr. Ball three of those to convince her to go to Iron Creek with him, the thought of which had been both mortifying and delightful to her. To spend so much time with him had been a delight, but she had changed the subject every time they spoke of her meeting her father. She could still hardly believe that they had found him after all this time, in the place where Mr. Ball would soon be making his home.

The entire situation was totally impossible, improbable, and yet it was real. Emily pressed her head against the cool glass of the window and wondered if anything in her life would ever be normal again. Just a few short months ago, she had not known Mr. Ball, her father had been no more than an occasional thought in her head, and she had been happy. Or she had at least thought she was happy. Now, she felt as though her world had been turned upside down – and to prove it, she was leaving its safe confines to go and face up to a past that her mother had kept hidden from her.

But though she was afraid of what she might learn, she couldn't help being glad that Mr. Ball had come with her. He had so much to do to get ready for his move across the country, yet he was prepared to come with her so she was not alone in a strange place. He had deftly maneuvered her through the station and onto the train, and he had dealt with the ticket inspector when he came through to check they had paid for their journey. She had watched him so she could learn how to speak to the waiters and porters, and the food in the restaurant car was delicious. It reminded her a little of the wonderful lunch she and Mr. Ball had shared at Parker's. Everything had changed since then.

Mr. Ball opened his eyes as the train slowed a little as they pulled into a station. "Was I asleep for long?" he asked.

"Only a few minutes," she assured him "We're not far from Cleveland. There was an announcement."

"I must have been sleeping for more than a few minutes then," he said with a smile. "You do not need to be polite, Miss Watson. If I am being an odious bore or neglecting you in any way, you must tell me so."

"You are tired. You raced back to see me, and have barely stopped since. You must need the rest."

"I do. It has been exciting and wonderful over the past few months, but sometimes it can be a little too much."

"I am sorry that I have caused you any trouble," Emily said, feeling guilty that his exhaustion was probably all her fault.

"Don't you dare tell me you are sorry. You are the reason I have had the most wonderful, challenging, and interesting time of my life. You must not ever apologize for giving me a case to really investigate. It made me see just how dull my life had become."

"Well, in that case, I am glad."

"You will love Iron Creek. It is the most beautiful place," he said happily. "I can't wait to show you our house. I'm hoping the mayor will have arranged a meeting with the gentleman who owns it while we are there. It would be wonderful to know that it is ours and that I can instruct the carpenter to start as soon as he is able."

"I am so glad that your Aunt Mary will be joining you," Emily said. "I am sure it would be hard on her to see you go otherwise." She would certainly find it hard to know that she would never see him again.

"I think she is more excited than I am, to tell you the truth. She fell under the spell of Iron Creek even more swiftly than I did." He smiled his gorgeous, crooked smile, and Emily wished that it was a memory of her happiness that had brought such pleasure to his heart, and not the happiness of his aunt. "She has already made fast friends with the other ladies there, and they will no doubt get into all manner of mischief together."

"It sounds like a very friendly place." Emily couldn't quite imagine that. Where she lived, most people looked out only for themselves. They couldn't afford to care too much for others around them. She and Marta barely knew any of their neighbors, despite the many months that they had been living in the cottage. Their community was the church, and without it and each other, they would live quite lonely lives.

"I've never known anywhere like it. Everyone seems to know everyone else, and though there are undoubtedly neighborly spats from time to time, nobody seems to hold a grudge. They pull together."

"Sounds a wonderful place to raise children," Emily said

wistfully, thinking how wonderful it would be to have Mr. Ball's children.

"I certainly hope so. My aunt has put in an order for a veritable army," he joked.

He stood up suddenly and pulled a large carpetbag from the rack overhead, which he placed on the seat beside Emily. "Before I forget, my aunt sent this for you." Curious, Emily opened the latch on the bag and pulled out a thick woolen coat and a pair of soft leather boots. "She was worried that you might not have a coat suitable for the cold weather in Minnesota, or warm boots."

"I can't accept these," she said, holding the coat up to look at. It was a rich, royal blue with gold buttons, and it was made of the softest, thickest wool Emily had ever touched. The boots would probably be a little too small, but they were made with exquisite stitching and the finest leather. "It is too much."

"I told Aunt Mary you would say that, which is why she insists that they are simply a loan while you are in Iron Creek."

"She is too kind, and I shall take very good care of them." Emily packed them carefully back into the bag and shook her head. "It is no wonder that you are such a kind and generous man when you had such a fine example to follow."

"Aunt Mary and Uncle Edward are the very finest people I know. They opened their hearts and their home to me and loved me as a son. I have always missed my parents, obviously, but I barely knew them when they died. I was lucky to have such warm and loving people to take me in, and I absolutely agree with you. I am the man I am because of their example." At that moment, his stomach rumbled loudly. He pulled out his pocket watch and then turned it to show her. "I think it is time we went for lunch."

The restaurant car was busy, but one of the waiters found them a table at the very end of the carriage. Mr. Ball offered to take the seat facing the wall of the train so that she could enjoy watching their fellow diners. It was just one of the many thoughtful gestures he made without even considering his own comfort that made her like him even more.

There was an elderly woman, dressed in black, with the largest hat Emily had ever seen. It was bedecked with feathers and sparkling beads, as was the bodice of her gown. She carried a large leather bag with her, and inside it was the smallest, fluffiest dog. It was so fluffy that it didn't look real, but it certainly yipped loudly enough when it was time for a tasty treat. The woman was rude to everyone and dismissive and complained about everything. Emily found her fascinating.

"Shall that be you one day?" Mr. Ball asked, turning discretely to see who had caught Emily's eye. His tone was almost flirtatious, which made Emily feel both incredibly flattered and self-conscious.

"Oh, I do hope not. Can you imagine how lonely her life

must have been to become so bitter and unhappy?" Emily said.

"I don't think becoming cantankerous and unpleasant will be your future, somehow," he said. His tone was light, but his eyes looked deep into hers. It made her insides turn to jelly.

"I shall certainly do my best to avoid it," she assured him nervously.

"I don't think you will need to try hard. People are drawn to kindness, I think." He looked away shyly, almost as if he had said more than he had meant to. Emily wanted to tell him she didn't mind but found herself unable to say a word.

Thankfully, the waiter appeared with their meal. For a few minutes, they were able to fill the rather awkward silence that had fallen between them by extolling the delights of their chosen courses. When they had eaten, they retired to their compartment, where Mr. Ball pulled out a book and began to read. Emily couldn't help thinking over what had happened at lunch. She knew what flirting looked like, though she had not indulged in it much herself, and she was sure that Mr. Ball had been flirting with her. Or had it just been her over-eager imagination seeing something that had not been there? She simply didn't know.

It certainly wasn't repeated throughout the rest of the journey. They stopped for the night in Chicago before taking the train to Duluth early the next morning. This train was not quite as well appointed as the one they had traveled on from

Boston, but it was comfortable enough. Once they reached Duluth, they then got on their final train, which would take them all the way to Iron Creek. As the train passed alongside Lake Superior, Emily gasped at the sight of so much calm, still water. As a Boston girl, she had visited the docks, of course, but they were nothing like this. As they made their way further north and west, mountains and trees dominated the landscape, and like Mr. Ball, Emily had to admit that seeing the Sawtooth Mountains was love at first sight.

She was exhausted when the train pulled into the station with a loud expulsion of steam and smoke that clouded the platform from view. As the fog cleared, she could see a neat and tidy station and several young lads waiting with barrows to help passengers with their luggage. Then the doors of the train began to open and the passengers descended, obscuring her view once more. Mr. Ball reached up for the carpetbag and handed it to her. "You might want to put these on," he said as he pulled on his own woolen coat and pulled out a pair of gloves.

She did as he'd suggested, swapping her own rather worn-out shoes for the soft leather boots and pulling on the heavy coat. It was delightfully warm. When Mr. Ball opened the door to their compartment, a blast of cold air struck Emily's face, making her gasp. "Oh, I see what you mean," she said with a laugh. "It is bitter."

"But it is so beautiful that a little cold can be forgiven, don't you think?"

"Oh, I do," she said fervently.

"Now, I have arranged for us to take rooms up at Pinewood Lodge, my friend's hotel, but if you would like to visit your father before we go up the mountain, I would be glad to accompany you there." Mr. Ball looked at her kindly, his voice and manner full of concern for her feelings.

"I think I should prefer to meet him when I am well rested," she said. "It will be a big moment for us both. It should not be snatched, and I should not be tired and grumpy."

"Then I shall fetch our bags and arrange transportation," Mr. Ball said happily. "I cannot wait for you to see the view from the hotel. It is quite spectacular."

CHAPTER 14

October 21, 1889, Iron Creek, Minnesota

Richard woke before the sun rose and made his way down to the stables. He saddled Bemised and went for a ride to work up an appetite for breakfast. He rode along the trails to the house he hoped would soon be his and Aunt Mary's. It looked just as wonderful in the dawn light as it had when they had first found it. He let himself dream a little about what living there would be like. He imagined himself chasing after his children, Aunt Mary watching from a rocking chair on the porch with a proud and happy expression. His wife came out of the door and called them all in to eat. He looked up and gazed into her perfect, blue eyes.

He shook his head. There had never been a face in his dreams until now. There had certainly never been such a vivid image of those gorgeous eyes that were almost violet in their intensity. And he knew those eyes. They were Miss Watson's eyes, and it had been Miss Watson's face. As he heaved himself onto Bemised's back, he realized that she was everything that he could ever want in a wife, and more. She was beautiful, gentle, and warm. And he loved her. He hadn't meant to. Every intention he might have held toward maintaining a professional relationship between them had crumbled in the face of the time he had spent with her.

But even if they had met in some other way, this was not the time to be pressing her about his own needs and wants. She had her own. She had much to come to terms with, and a meeting with her long-lost father to face. He would not add to her burdens. And why should she leave Boston, the place that she had called home her entire life? She had connections there that were deeper than anything he could imagine. His roots were firmly entwined around his aunt and uncle. Hers were sunk deep in the earth of Boston. Asking her to leave would be too much – and he could not go back there.

He had found everything he had ever wanted in Iron Creek. The only thing it had not provided him was Miss Watson. Her feelings for the place seemed to have been as immediate as his own, but they could change in a moment if the meeting with her father did not go well. She might wish to leave town and never return once she heard his side of the story. And as Richard did not know what Mayor Winston wanted to tell Miss Watson, he had no idea how she would react. All he could do was hope and pray that all would be well.

On his return to the hotel, he took a quick bath and rinsed the grime of travel and the smell of horse from his body. He dressed with care and went down to the dining room. Miss Watson was already there, early as always. She looked up at him and smiled as he approached the table she was sitting so patiently at.

"Good morning. You look well rested," she said.

"As do you," he said, politely nodding his head before taking the seat opposite her. "Would you like me to send word to Mayor Winston that we will join him today?"

"I would," she said cautiously. "But would you be terribly offended if I spoke with him alone?"

"Not at all," Richard assured her. "I would have been happy to accompany you if you wished to have my support, but I will wait in the gig if that is what you prefer."

"There is no need to wait. Perhaps we can arrange a time and a place for us to meet, away from the mayor's house? Just in case."

He gave her what he hoped was a reassuring smile. "I think that is a fine idea. The church might be a good place. There is a path that goes down to the creek from there. If you need somewhere to go and think, the creek is the perfect spot."

"It sounds ideal." She was a little pale and clearly afraid, but she straightened her spine and tried to look confident about what was about to transpire. "I just wish I had even an inkling of what I might learn today."

"Whatever he tells you, Miss Watson, I believe it will be the truth. He is an honest man. I like him very much."

After breakfast, they walked to the stables together. Miss Watson clung to his arm tightly. He had never known her to be so anxious, and he wished there was more he could do to ease her mind. He could not imagine the thoughts that must be troubling her, the fears of what she might learn. He helped her up into the gig and was strangely delighted when she continued to hold his arm, her slender body cuddled up close to his own. He wished that they might enjoy many such moments in the future, though preferably without Miss Watson being petrified when they did.

He drove them carefully down the mountain and into the town, pointing out the bakery and telling her of the delicious pastries that were sold there. "As good as any in Boston," he said. "Aunt Mary grew overly fond of them when she was here. Perhaps I could go to the bakery and purchase us a picnic lunch? We could eat it down by the creek. You need not say a word to me if you do not wish to."

"I think that would be lovely," she said. "And I will tell you all that happens. Perhaps not immediately after, but you deserve to know how all of this ends after everything you have done for me. I can never repay you for the money you have spent, bringing me here, taking me to Parker's, the hansom cabs, and all your time."

"Knowing you are happy and have the answers you need is more than enough payment, Miss Watson. You made me see that I had settled for a life that did not make me happy. You shook me up and made me see that there is better out there, for all of us, if we are brave enough to take that terrifying first step."

"I am glad you feel that way. I have no idea how you think I did all that, but I am flattered that you credit me with such things."

Richard pulled the gig to a halt outside Mayor Winston's house. "Is this it?" she asked, her face blanching even whiter. Richard nodded. "I knew his family was wealthy, but a house like this? No wonder he thought Mom wasn't good enough for him."

"We don't know that he thought that at all. But only he can tell you. I'll not be far away, at the bakery, or visiting Mr. Drayton at his yard at the end of Main Street. But if not, I shall see you at the creek at midday?"

"Midday," she echoed softly, her eyes wide as she continued to stare up at the grand house.

EMILY STARED up at the house. Harriet had said that her father's family had been wealthy, and perhaps in comparison with some Boston mansions it was a modest enough place, but it was a palace to her eyes. It stood out among the other houses on Main Street, even though many of them were very fine. Her hand shaking, she opened the gate and began to slowly walk up the path. She saw the dark, prickled stems of rosebushes in the borders and wondered what colors they were. Mom had always loved cream roses.

Stepping up onto the porch, she raised her hand to take the lion's head knocker. But she couldn't bring herself to grasp it. Her entire body was quivering and her belly was a mass of writhing worms. She took a deep breath, exhaled sharply, and took the knob firmly. She rapped on the door three times, stepped back, and waited, hardly daring to breathe.

The door was opened by a rather rotund man with a kind face and a furrowed brow. His eyes were red-rimmed, and he looked as if he had been crying. He opened his mouth as if he intended to speak, then closed it again. Tears began to fall down his cheeks. "Oh, my dear," he managed to mutter. "You are the very image of my Janet, the very image. Come in, come in."

Emily followed him inside and waited while he closed the door. He turned to her with a strange smile on his face. "Oh, let me look at you. You are the very image of your mother," he repeated. "I can hardly believe that you are here. If I am honest, I was rather taken aback when dear Richard said that you existed. I never knew. I never knew." He spoke rapidly, but with real emotion. Emily trusted him immediately. His feelings were clearly sincere.

"You did not know about me?" she asked.

"Not until Richard told me of you, no."

"I don't understand any of this," Emily said. He took her into his parlor and sat her down.

"I'm not sure that I do, and sadly it would seem the few people who could answer all our questions no longer live," he said sadly.

Emily saw a tea tray on a table and gestured at it. "Shall I pour?" she asked. He nodded.

Her hands were still shaking as she picked up the teapot. He gave her a kind smile though tears continued to pour down his cheeks. "I can barely see, and you are all aquiver," he said. "What a pair we make."

Emily put the teapot down for a moment, then tried again. This time, it was easier. She poured them each a cup of tea. "Do you take sugar?"

"I did not get this belly from a healthy abstinence," he joked, patting his belly. "Janet would be ashamed of me, letting myself go like this. Two, please."

Emily used the shiny silver tongs to add two lumps to his cup and stirred it thoroughly before handing it to him. She picked up her own cup and took a sip. "Might I ask why you left my mother? I know the two of you were married."

"The very best day of my life," Mayor Winston said with a fond smile. He closed his eyes for a moment as if he were reliving it all in his head. "I cannot tell you how many times I have thought of that day. I thought that once we were married, my family would accept everything. I was wrong."

"I don't understand?"

"I will tell you the whole sorry tale, as far as I can tell it. There are gaps that perhaps only dear Janet or my parents might have been able to answer for us, but I think that we may be able to work those out between us once you know my side of the matter."

Emily put her cup and saucer down and perched on the edge of her seat. "How did you meet?"

"I was at Harvard, studying history. I was fascinated by England, the motherland for my family I suppose you might call it. I longed to travel there, and my family had promised that they would pay for me to do so after I completed my degree. I could hardly wait to get away. I was as unlike the rest of my family as anyone can be. They valued wealth and power over everything. My brother will likely be the next governor of Massachusetts, thanks to the connections and money they accrued throughout their lives."

"Goodness," Emily said. "Yet you fell in love with my mother?"

"Indeed, I did. It was a terrible cliché I suppose, I fell in love with the help. Your mother was a maid in my parent's townhouse. I adored her from the first moment I saw her. She was the only person to ever show me even an ounce of affection in all my life in that terrible place."

"I see," Emily said. "No wonder your parents did not approve."

"Indeed, they did not. Such a thing, should it get out, would have caused a great scandal and brought disgrace upon the entire family. We weren't so wealthy that we could get away with doing whatever we liked. There were rules to follow, and my parents were not going to let a foolish boy ruin their plans."

"But you were married in the eyes of the Lord?" Emily said aghast.

"We were. And as you are here, you know that it was consummated. There were no legal or religious grounds for a divorce, and my family is Catholic."

"My mother was, too. As am I," Emily said.

He nodded. "Yes, we attended mass together many times. So, you can understand why there could be no divorce. But there could also never be a word about my marriage to your mother ever uttered again. It must not ever get out."

"Your parents sound horrible," Emily said frankly.

"They were like the rest of their social circle. I cannot say I liked them, and I know they disliked me as I was not like them. But they were only doing what they had been raised to do by their parents, in turn. I am glad you grew up away from them and their insidious influence."

"But how did they keep you from one another?"

"My father had business interests all over the world. He had an upcoming trip to London and said that it was time I went along to learn the ropes. Fool that I am, I could not see anything strange about such a request, and to go to London was my dearest dream. I kissed Janet goodbye, thinking I would be returning to her side in a matter of months. And I never saw her again. I should never have left her. I should have taken her with me. We could have started new lives in England and never seen my family ever again. But my mother assured me that she would take care of your mother, that she would teach her how to be a lady at our estate, near Philadelphia."

"My mother never told me about living in Philadelphia," Emily said, surprised.

"That is because she never left Boston," Mayor Winston said sadly. "My mother said that she would send for her, and so your mother waited." He paused. "I am now moving into the realms of conjecture because I can only tell my side of what happened next. I can only assume that my parents told your mother something similar."

"What did they tell you?"

"My mother wrote to me in London, telling me that my beloved Janet had died of influenza," he said starkly. Tears streaked down his cheeks once more. He dabbed them away with a handkerchief. "They even had a plot in our family cemetery made for her, but for some reason or another, the headstone was never erected. Mother said the stonemason kept making mistakes, but there was a freshly dug grave. Can you imagine going to such lengths?"

"They told you she was dead? Did you not think to come to Boston and check?"

"Why would I?" he wailed. "I believed that she had gone to live with my family. When your own family tells you that your wife is dead, you believe them."

"And they probably told her the same thing, which is why your letters stopped just before I was born and why she kept your watch and could never bring herself to speak of you. Her grief must have been unbearable."

"If it was like mine, then yes, but we had no choice but to bear it. She had you to raise, and I felt honor bound to do something to honor her memory. I couldn't stay in Philadelphia, and I had no desire to return to Boston, where there was a memory of her on every corner. So when a friend suggested moving here, I took the chance. I started again, but I have thought of her every day." He reached into his pocket, pulled out a miniature, and handed it to Emily. The face staring back at her was as familiar as her own.

"Mom," she said with a sigh, beginning to cry, too. It was such a terribly sad story, but suddenly everything about her life made perfect sense. "Your roses…" she started to say.

"Are cream. Her favorites," he said softly.

CHAPTER 15

October 21, 1889, Iron Creek, Minnesota

It was almost too much to take in. Emily knew that there were people who would go to any length to get what they wanted in life, but to ruin two young people's lives so completely and leave them in mourning for the rest of their lives seemed barbaric. That it had been done to them by family, even more so.

"You never married again?" she asked Mayor Winston.

"No." His response was terse. He sounded as if he were offended by the mere thought of such a thing. Emily's heart went out to him. He had lived as lonely a life as her mother had.

"Neither did she," Emily said sadly.

"Richard told me that your mother passed away," he said tentatively. "I am so sorry for your loss."

"She did her best. Worked every hour to keep a roof over our heads and food in our bellies," Emily said. The more she thought about the privations they had faced, the angrier she got. Her mother and Mayor Winston could have led happy lives, together, here. They would not have been an embarrassment to his family. She could have had a father, and they would have been happy. There had been no need to break them all apart.

The mayor jumped to his feet and began pacing in front of the fire. "I wish I had come back to Boston. I wish I hadn't trusted them," he said desperately. "They let me lay flowers on her grave every day until I left. How could they do that? How could they deceive us both in such a terrible way? Was their standing in Society truly so important that they could bring such pain to us both?"

"You know them," Emily reminded him. "I do not. But I grew up knowing men that would murder their own families if it meant they could get ahead in life. Ambition is a dangerous and heady poison."

"I cannot agree with you more," Mayor Winston said. "I am saddened that you grew up that way, though."

"It seems your upbringing was not so different," Emily said wryly. "I think people are much the same wherever they fall in life. There will always be those content with their lot and those who want for more. And there will always be those who will convince themselves that any act is justified if it serves their purpose."

"You are wise for one so young, Miss Watson." He paused as he said the name. "Though, given you were both conceived and born in wedlock, I suppose your name should truly be Winston."

"I suppose it should," Emily said. "Though I do hope you will not be offended if I keep my name. It is a little bit of her that I carry with me."

"I understand entirely," he said, looking at her fondly. "Though I would be honored if you would let me call you Emily. And you must call me Logan, I think it might be a little early for you to consider me as your Papa, but I do hope that one day you will."

"Perhaps in time," Emily said softly. "I am glad to know you, and to know that you didn't leave us through choice."

"And I am glad to know that your mother lives on in our child. I know I said it before, but you are very much like her. You have her eyes and that stubborn tilt to your head."

The clock on the mantel chimed, and Emily glanced at it. It was a quarter to twelve already. Time had passed more quickly than she had expected it to. If she did not hurry, she would be late meeting Mr. Ball at the creek. She stood up. "I think I should be on my way now," she said gently. "I think we both have much to think about. But I would like to call on you again before I go home to Boston, if you would like that?"

"I should be delighted," Logan said, beaming at her and taking her hands in his. His were warm, and soft, except for the calluses on the fingers where he held his pen. She smiled back at him and leaned over and kissed his cheek. He flushed beet red, clearly delighted.

"I shall see you soon," she promised.

He saw her out of the house, and she made her way to the path by the church that Mr. Ball had told her of. It would not do to leave him there alone, thinking she had forgotten or that she did not want to tell him what had occurred. She walked swiftly, glad of the fine boots and thick coat that Mrs. Ball had lent her. The path was hard, the air cold. It seemed strange to Emily. If it was this bitter in Boston, there would be snow, yet there was none on the ground, just icy puddles and glistening frost everywhere.

The path led through woodland. The fir trees were still green, though there were plenty of icy, crisp leaves that had fallen from other trees underfoot. Occasionally, she heard a rustling in the distance and the odd snap of a twig, but she didn't see what was making the noises. It made her a little anxious, wondering if it were a wild animal or someone lying in wait for an unsuspecting wanderer. She laughed out loud. What could possibly be more dangerous here than it was in Boston?

She emerged from the trees and immediately saw the creek. The waters were fast and looked far deeper than she had expected. She looked up and down the riverbank, hoping to see Mr. Ball. She prayed that he had not already left, fed up with waiting for her. But if he had, surely he would have passed her on the path? She noticed a wisp of smoke to her left, so she walked along the path that led in that direction.

Around a bend in the creek, she found Mr. Ball, warming his hands over a small fire that had a kettle hanging over it on a rather flimsy-looking tripod that must have been made from sticks he had found in the woods. He was sitting on a cushion placed on a thick fur rug, and there was a pile of thick woolen blankets beside him. There was a second cushion beside him and a large picnic basket between them. She couldn't help wondering how he had managed to transport everything without any assistance.

Hearing her footsteps, he looked up and smiled at her. "Late, for once," he teased. She felt the telltale heat rise up through her chest, neck, and face and knew she was blushing. She ducked her head and took a seat on the cushion beside him. He handed her a thick fur blanket, and she tucked it around her body tightly.

"How did it go?" he asked. He took two cups out of the basket and placed them on a flattish rock by the fire, followed by a small teapot. "You look much less, I don't know, emotional than I was expecting." Emily watched as he used an old cloth to take the kettle from the tripod and filled the pot. "There are leaves already in there," he said with a grin.

"Very resourceful," she noted. "As to your questions, as

you said, he is a good and honest man. I found no reason to doubt his telling of the story." She quickly recounted everything Logan had told her.

"My goodness," he said when she had done so. "I could not have predicted that. Poor Mayor Winston, coming from a family like that." He lifted the pot and poured them each a cup of warming tea.

"Yes, they ruined all of our lives," Emily said. She wrapped her gloved fingers around her cup, relishing the heat. "They didn't have a care for anyone but themselves. And to preserve nothing more than a place in Society."

"It is quite horrific. I noticed that you called him Logan. Does that mean that the two of you are friends, at least?"

"I think so," Emily said with a smile. "He had no inkling that my mother was with child when he left for England, so I believe I have come as a rather nice surprise for him. He seems delighted that there is still a little of my mother left in the world."

"And how do you feel about him now?"

"I like him. I think it will take me a long time to adjust to the idea of having a father, but I am glad that I do."

Richard pulled some neatly wrapped packages from the basket and laid them between them on the rug. Emily took one and unwrapped it. It was a small pie that was still a little warm. She sniffed it. "Mmm, beef and beer," she said happily. "My favorite."

"I have a dreadful sweet tooth, so these are my favorites," Mr. Ball said, unwrapping a selection of pastries. He began to rummage in the bottom of the picnic basket. "But I thought it best if we had a savory course to start. I have a knife, plates, and even forks in here, somewhere." It took him a few moments, but he was soon brandishing the cutlery he sought. Emily took out the plates and waited as he cut the pie in half and put a piece on each plate.

Emily had to admit that she had never tasted a pie so delicious. She wasn't sure if it was because it was warming on such a cold day or if it was because she was eating it with Mr. Ball, or simply that it was the finest pie she had ever had. "This came from the bakery?" she asked.

"Yes. He's a marvel, isn't he? I don't think there's a finer baker anywhere – and I have traveled all over this fair country of ours."

When the pie was devoured, they shared out the pastries. Neither of them spoke as they ate, but they both made murmurs of delight as they savored the delicate pastry, the sweet fillings, and the creamy richness of the French-style patisserie. "These are even better than the dessert at Parker's," Emily declared.

"I have to agree. Wesley Baker is an artist in the kitchen," Mr. Ball said fervently.

"His name is Baker, and he is a baker?" Emily said with a grin.

"It is rather apt, isn't it? Though not uncommon."

"Were his family all bakers, too?"

"I suppose they must have been at some point, to garner such a surname, but he learned his trade from a French man in Minneapolis."

"Well, we are blessed that he did," Emily said, shivering ever so slightly. "Is there more tea? I'm a little chilly."

"There is, but perhaps it would be best for us to head back to town," Mr. Ball suggested. "It was probably not one of my finest ideas, having a picnic in Minnesota in late October."

"It was a fine idea, and I have enjoyed it very much," Emily assured him. "But a walk back to town, carrying all of this, will no doubt warm us both back up again."

She began to pack the plates, cutlery, and the paper that had wrapped the food up into the picnic basket. Mr. Ball stood up and disappeared behind the large rock behind them for a moment. He emerged with a small barrow.

"Ah," Emily said. "That was how you managed to bring everything here on your own."

"I borrowed it from Alec at the smithy. I'll need to return it on our way back."

Carefully, they packed everything up, then Mr. Ball doused the fire. They walked in companionable silence back through the woods. Suddenly, Mr. Ball stopped and put his finger to his lips to indicate that Emily should be silent. She stopped moving, and he slowly and quietly set down the barrow. He moved close enough to her that she could feel the warmth of his body behind her, then pointed into the trees over her shoulder. She followed the line of his finger, hardly daring to even breathe. A majestic stag stood no more than ten yards away from them. Emily bit her lip to stop herself from sighing at the sight of him. They stood silently until he moved away.

"My goodness," Emily gasped. "I have never seen anything like that before."

"I must confess that I haven't either," Mr. Ball said, still staring after the magnificent beast. "He has quite taken my breath away."

She smiled, delighted by his boyish enthusiasm. She wished that she could be with him always, but that could never be if he intended to move here. Her life was in Boston. She had not seen any mills or factories in Iron Creek, and she did not know how to do anything else. Besides, he had given her no reason to think that he might want her to do such a thing. After all, he was her attorney. He had done all she had hired him to do. There need be no further contact between them once she left Iron Creek and returned home.

The thought of that made her unbearably sad, but she tried not to show it as they made their way to Iron Creek, where they returned the borrowed barrow to Alec Jenks, a gentle giant of a man who Emily liked immediately. She had not met a single unpleasant person in her time in Iron Creek. Oh, she was sure some must exist, but everyone had been very welcoming, just as Mr. Ball had described them. She wondered what they would think when they found out who she really was. Would they judge her mother and Mayor Winston or lay the blame for their unintended estrangement where it belonged – on the Winston family and their unbridled ambitions?

CHAPTER 16

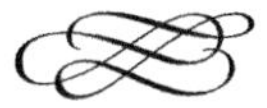

October 25, 1889, Iron Creek, Minnesota

The pile of rumpled clothing on his bed made Richard frown. He should have taken everything out of his bag upon his arrival. He knew better than to just leave a bag packed throughout a journey. Now, he would need to send his last shirt down to be laundered and pressed and hope that it would be back in time before the train left in the morning. Apprehensively, he made his way down to the laundry room, where a young girl he'd not met before was stirring a vast copper pot. She bobbed him a curtsey. "May I help you, Sir?" she asked.

"I have been a fool. I should have unpacked my clothes properly. I thought I had taken all of my shirts out at least, but I found this one – my last one – tucked away in the bottom of my bag. Would you be able to clean and press it?

The only problem is that my train leaves at eight o'clock in the morning. Would it be too much trouble?"

"No trouble at all, Sir," she assured him, quickly taking a sniff of it. "After all, it is not dirty. I'm right, aren't I? You've not worn it since it was last laundered. It smells of starch and soap."

"No, I've not worn it," he said, feeling peculiarly embarrassed that a stranger had just sniffed his shirt and that he was in this predicament in the first place.

"I am sure I can press the wrinkles out of it and have it back to you before you finish your dinner tonight," she said.

"You are an angel, Miss…?"

"Edie Porter," she said with a smile. "I believe you spoke with my brother-in-law about the old house on the Harding trail. I am so glad that someone wants to live there. It could be such a lovely family home."

"I certainly hope so, Miss Porter. For I signed the papers that make it mine this very morning."

Glad that his dilemma was in capable hands, Richard made his way upstairs to the bar. Mayor Winston was waiting for him. He had a glass of brandy at his lips, which he quickly put down to hold out a hand in greeting. The men shook hands, and Richard suddenly remembered why his handshake had seemed so familiar when they had first met. His hands were just like Miss Watson's, and his grip was much the same, too. He couldn't help grinning at the observation.

"What is it?" the mayor asked, anxiously starting to check his person for spilled food stains or some such.

"Oh, it is not you. At least not precisely you." The mayor gave him a puzzled look as they both took their seats. "It is just that Miss Watson, well, she shakes hands much the same way that you do."

"My goodness, I should never have thought such a thing might be inheritable," Mayor Winston said with a chuckle. "I would wager that my hands are probably a little softer than hers, given the life she has had to lead. I hate that she and her mother were forced to live in poverty because my family was so cruel."

"You've spent some time with her, I believe, in the past few days?"

"I have. She is quite charming and much more forgiving than she should be. I only wish that she could stay here longer so we might truly get to know one another, but she is insistent that she must return to Boston and her life there. I think she is afraid she might lose her position at the mill."

"It is certainly something that would be a concern. There is not much work available in Boston at the moment for a girl who has lost a place through her own actions," Richard said.

"I'd not have her go short. I would gladly pay her rent there and her keep here, but she will have none of it. She is as proud as her mother. She never liked to take a dime from me, either." He gave a sad, fond smile and took another sip of his brandy. "I shall miss her as much as I miss her mother. She is a very special young lady."

Richard did not say anything. He simply nodded his agreement that Miss Watson was special and that he would miss her. Throughout the journey he had taken with her, he had known that there would come a time when they would part, but he was not yet ready for it. His job was done. Father and daughter were reunited, and if Mayor Winston could not convince her to stay in Iron Creek, then what hope did he have in persuading her?

Jonny appeared in the doorway and beckoned to the two men. "Our table is ready in the dining room," he said. Richard and Mayor Winston stood up and walked toward him. "And the women are waiting and hungry."

The dining room was quiet that night, but a large table had been placed across the very center of the room. Andy sat in his wheelchair at one end of the table. Amy was sitting at his left, and Jonny's wife, Cassie, was at his right. Jonny moved to the chair beside her and indicated that Mayor Winston should take the seat at the end. Miss Watson was to his left, next to an empty seat, which Richard took after greeting all the ladies with a polite nodding bow and Andy with a firm handshake.

A waiter appeared with a bottle of champagne and poured glasses for each of them. Mayor Winston stood up and raised his glass. "We are so glad that you are all here to enjoy Emily's final evening with us in Iron Creek," he said proudly. "We are both grateful for all your kindnesses to her, since arriving here, and we feel," he glanced at Miss Watson, who smiled and nodded at him, "that it is time that we told you why she is here."

"I presumed that Richard took our advice and actually answered some of those letters he had with him last time," Jonny said with a cheeky wink.

Richard shook his head. "Not exactly," he said. "But I did make Miss Watson's acquaintance because of those letters." She smiled up at him, and he felt the imminent pain of never seeing her again once he took her back to Boston. He was not sure he would be able to bear it.

Mayor Winston tapped his glass with a teaspoon, drawing everyone's attention away from their intrigued mutterings and back to himself. "As I was saying," he said pointedly. "It is time to tell you why she is here. Emily is my daughter."

The look of shock on everyone present's face was almost a delight. Richard couldn't help laughing at his new friends. They stared first at Mayor Winston, then at Miss Watson, then at one another. Jonny was the first to find his tongue, of course. "But, how?" he asked.

"A long time ago," Andy started. "A boy and a girl fell in love, and then they had a baby."

Everyone laughed at his quip. "And not far from the truth," Miss Watson said shyly. "Though there were a few twists and turns after that part of the story. The wonderful part is that I finally know who my father is, and he knows me." She stood up and pressed a kiss to Mayor Winston's cheek. He flushed beet red, obviously as pleased as punch at her action.

Everyone stood and raised their glasses. "To a family reunited," Jonny said.

They all drank, then took their seats as the first course appeared. For a few moments, everyone talked among themselves, but suddenly, Amy turned to Miss Watson. "But surely, that means that you will be coming back, won't you?"

"I don't know," Miss Watson said a little sadly. "I do like it here, very much, but my life is in Boston, and it would take me a year to save enough to make the trip here – and that is only if I am able to keep my job."

"Oh," Amy said softly. "I did not think of that, and I should have. I know all too well how hard it is to find your way in the world."

"I did offer my daughter a room in my house and promised I would help her to get settled here, but she is not yet ready for that," Mayor Winston said sagely. "I think it wise, too, that we get to know each other better before she takes such a big step. I shall make a point of visiting Boston as often as I can, so I may need to appoint a deputy mayor to act in my stead when I am gone."

"I would be glad to put my name forward," Jonny said boldly.

"I was thinking our dear blacksmith friend Alec might be a possibility. He's in the town and has a steady head."

"He would be a fine choice," Cassie said, grinning at her husband's ambition and patting his hand affectionately. "And I am sure the rest of the town will agree."

Jonny shook his head as if in disbelief at his wife's treachery, then laughed. Everyone else laughed with him.

The rest of the meal was delicious, and the conversation barely stopped throughout the entire evening. When the time came to send Mayor Winston, Andy, and Amy back to Iron Creek, Richard was sure that he had made the right choice to move here. He only wished Miss Watson could see that, too. He watched her being hugged by Amy and Cassie and teased by Andy and Jonny and couldn't help wondering if she realized all she was giving up by returning to Boston. They had all taken to her so quickly, and she to them.

As the carriage trundled down the mountain, Jonny and Cassie said goodnight, leaving Miss Watson and Richard alone on the porch. "That was a wonderful evening," she said with a sigh, leaning against the balustrade.

"Yes, it was," he agreed. "There could be many more of them if you would just stay."

"I have explained this to my father, and to everyone at the table tonight. I simply cannot. My life is in Boston. As it is, I may not have a position to return to. This trip, everything we've learned, can you not see that my life has been quite turned upside down? I need to get back to what is familiar, to what I know, so that I can make some sense of it all."

It was the answer he had expected, but it still stung to hear her say it. "I can understand that," he said sadly. "But I don't think my life will ever be quite the same again, either. You've rather turned it upside down."

"*You've* done that. You came to Iron Creek and fell in love with it long before you met me and had to start chasing after my long-lost father," she said, her tone a little forced as she tried to keep the conversation light.

"That is true, I suppose," he said. He looked at her, taking in the lines of her face and her long, slender arms, and realized that she must be half frozen. He pulled off his jacket and draped it around her shoulders. "Perhaps we should go inside and talk in the bar, perhaps?"

"No, I should go to bed," she said. "I am tired, and we have a long journey ahead of us."

He walked her to the bottom of the grand staircase. She took the first two steps, then turned back to him and took off his jacket and handed it to him. "Thank you," she said softly, then turned to go upstairs.

"Wait," he said, a little more loudly than he'd intended. She looked back at him. "Is there nothing I can say, is there nothing I can do, to convince you to stay here? I truly believe you will be happier here, and your father is over the moon to know you."

She shook her head sadly. "No, there is nothing. I am as

out of place here as my mother would have been in Logan's family. I don't know if that will be the case forever, but it is now."

He watched her walk up the rest of the staircase and turn onto the corridor where her room was. "If I asked you to marry me, would that make you stay?" he whispered a little sadly, then he made his way up to his own bedchamber.

CHAPTER 17

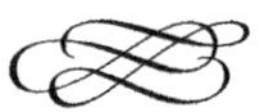

November 7, 1889, Boston, Massachusetts

Emily knew that Mr. Ball and his aunt would be leaving on the train for Iron Creek in the morning, and this time it would be forever. She knew that their belongings would follow them a few days later. While they had been on the train back to Boston, he'd told her about their plans and how excited he was about starting his new life – and how terrible he felt that he had left his aunt alone to make the preparations for their journey. It had made her realize that she would be unlikely to ever see him again.

He had still not let her make any manner of payment for the services he had so generously provided. She could still hardly believe that not only was her father alive but that he wanted her to be a large part of his life. She owed Mr. Ball everything. So, upon her return, she had borrowed money from Marta, Marjorie, and a couple of the other girls at the mill so that she could feel that she had paid her dues and that the matter was settled in full. Yet, he still would not accept it. Rather than returning her money to her in person, he had sent it back using one of the many lads in the city who would deliver anything, anywhere for a penny.

She had been surprised by how much it had hurt that he had not found the time to see her before he departed. She reminded herself that she was just a client, like any other, and Mr. Ball did not have the time to visit everyone he had ever known, but there had been a closeness between them, she was sure of it. Or perhaps she had simply seen what she wanted to because to have his friendship and his affection would mean the world to her. Mr. Ball had become as vital to her as Marta was, as Harriet and her family were. And she would miss him terribly.

"You could go to Iron Creek," Marta reminded her. "Your father's offer would mean that you could get to know him and be closer to Mr. Ball. Perhaps in time, he might see you as you see him?"

"I could not," Emily said sadly. "Though every selfish bone in my body wishes to do just that, I will not get in his way. He has a new life to build, and he does not need a foolish girl hanging on his every word."

"Pshaw," Marta snorted. "I know you do not believe me, but that man has spent a small fortune helping you find your father and would not accept a penny to repay him. Such things are not what a man does for a woman he has no interest in."

"Marta, I cannot leave. Even if what you say is true. What if things with my father go wrong? What if I find myself stranded there? I will have left everything I know behind me and will be so far away that I cannot imagine ever having enough money to pay for my ticket to return. I would have given up my job and the little security that you and I have managed to win for ourselves – and for what?"

"The chance to have a relationship with your father," Marta pointed out. "And a chance to win the man you love – and do not try to deny that you love him."

"Oh, I don't deny it," Emily said. "I do love him."

It felt strangely freeing to say it out loud. Marta gave her a hug and a look filled with compassion. "I must go to bed or I will never be up for work in the morning, but we can talk on this more when you get in from work tomorrow if you want to."

"Thank you, Marta. I sometimes wonder what I would do without you."

"But you are not in love with me, so chasing after me anywhere in the country would not be such a matter of pride," she said sagely.

"Would you follow me anywhere?" Emily asked. "Because I would follow you. I cannot imagine my life without you in it."

"Of course I would," Marta said. "Even if it is to the icy

wastes of Minnesota." She grinned and kissed Emily's cheek, then went up to bed.

Emily thought about that, alone in their tiny back room once the sound of Marta's footsteps overhead came to an end, as she got into bed. Her friend was right. She would not have a moment's hesitation in following Marta if she were offered a chance at a new life somewhere else. Her feelings for her friend would not be questioned or thought strange. Mr. Ball was also a friend, but everything was different. She could not even go to him and say goodbye. Such a thing would be utterly inappropriate.

She banked the fire and blew out the lamp in the back room, then went into the kitchen. The stove was still lit, keeping the room warm. She put some water on the stove to heat so she could wash the dishes before turning in. When Marta returned from the bakery in the afternoons, she always made sure there was food ready when Emily returned from the mill. Emily tidied up after Marta went to bed. On Wednesdays and Sundays, they cooked and cleaned up together. On Wednesdays, they had the Tolman children for tea, too. Occasionally, they both went to the Tolmans' for lunch after church on Sunday. Their lives were well-ordered and offered Emily security. She couldn't leave all that behind, not for her father, and most certainly not for a man who had probably almost forgotten her already.

Though she tried to be quiet as she washed the dishes, dried them and put them away, there was always some noise, and because of it she almost didn't notice a very soft knock on the door. She looked up, but thinking it had probably been her putting a bowl down too hard, she went back to her chores. Another, slightly louder knock came a few moments later. This time, Emily was sure that it was the door. Glancing up the stairs and listening for any movement, she prayed that it hadn't woken Marta and cautiously opened the door.

She was surprised to see Mr. Ball standing in the darkness. "Whatever are you doing here?" she asked, her voice a hissing whisper. "It is late, and it isn't safe here for a man like you."

"But it is for a young woman like yourself?" he whispered back with a grin.

"I don't leave the house at this time of night," she retorted, ushering him inside. "We must be quiet. Marta has gone to bed."

"I remember that she is early to bed, and I am thankful for it. I got Aunt Mary to switch to the bakery where Miss Pauling works, and she has been delighted with the quality of the bread and cakes."

"You did not come here to talk about Marta's baking," Emily said, frowning at him. "And you clearly had little time to speak with me, or you wouldn't have sent your fee back with a messenger boy." She was delighted to see him so she could say goodbye properly, but she was also angry that he would take such a risk as to walk around the neighborhood at night. Heaven only knew what might have befallen him.

"You are not mad about that?" he said, his eyes twinkling.

She sighed heavily and rolled her eyes at him. "You cannot always rely upon your charm to dispel my wrath," she warned him.

"I should hope not," he said jovially. "But, please, do not be angry with me over that. I returned the money because I know you cannot afford to pay it. And because your father insisted that he reimburse me in full. He really is delighted that he has a daughter, you know."

"Perhaps if you had included a letter to that end with the money," Emily said, "I would not have been so cross."

He chuckled. "If I am totally honest, I had not yet received your father's telegram to that end at the time. In truth, I returned it because I simply could not ethically take it. You see, I did not take your case to make money. I took your case because I liked you. I liked that you were brave enough to write to a complete stranger who was advertising for a wife." He raised an eyebrow and gave her a cheeky grin. "I do not know a single woman who would do such a thing – except you."

"You liked me?"

"I did. I still do, in fact. It has been the dullest week of my life since I dropped you here after our journey – simply because you were not in it. And though we have been busy every minute, your face kept flashing before my eyes. And every night, I longed to rush here, to beg you to reconsider your decision to remain in Boston, to beg you to take up your father's offer so we can get to know each other even better. I kept wishing you would call on us to offer your assistance, or perhaps to just shout at me for returning your money."

"I am busy, too," she pointed out. "I work all day, and it is not safe for anyone to be wandering around this part of Boston late at night. Even if I had wanted to call on you, I am sure that you can see how very inappropriate such a thing would be. I know I am not a Society Miss, but it is never a woman's place to call upon a gentleman."

"And so, I have come to you," he said simply, completely ignoring her indignation. "Miss Watson, I have missed you very much. Have you not missed me, not even a little bit?"

"You are teasing me, and that is unfair when you leave for Minnesota tomorrow and I will never see you again," Emily said, feeling suddenly rather awkward and overwhelmed by the way he was quite clearly flirting with her.

"It does not have to be that way," he said. "Take up your father's offer. Stay with him for a while, then you will see me every day. I want to see you every day. Don't you want that, too? I know that you have feelings for me. Perhaps they are not as strong as mine are for you, but I am certain they are there."

"As strong as yours?" Emily queried. "But you–"

"I love you," he interrupted her. "I want to marry you if you'll have me."

"No, I cannot believe this is real," Emily said stubbornly. A part of her longed to simply say yes, to pack up her meager belongings that very minute and go with him. But she could not. She simply could not trust what he was saying to her. "You're saying I should marry you and move to Iron Creek, just like that? Without there ever having been an inkling of this until now?"

"That is precisely what I am saying," he said. "Don't you think I wanted to say something? You were my client. It would have been both impolite and unprofessional of me to push my feelings onto you while I was working for you. But surely you knew? I cannot believe that you did not feel it, the connection between us is too strong."

"Mr. Ball, I cannot just agree to marry you," Emily said sadly. "I absolutely do feel the connection between us, but like my parents, we come from very different worlds. I could never fit into your world. Can you not see that?"

"Here, perhaps," Mr. Ball said simply. "I agree that people that come from such different worlds as ourselves might find it hard here, but Iron Creek is not Boston. Did you not see that such matters as how much money you have or what place in Society you possess simply are not concerns the people have there? We could be happy there. I know it."

"You think that, but even in Iron Creek, there will be

rules of who should be with who," she said sadly, resigned to the way things were in the world.

"Did you not listen to all of those stories that Jonny and Andy told us about all the people in town who found love through advertisements? None of them cared about class or money. They simply fell in love, and nobody in town looks down on them for it. That could be us – if you would just let it." His eyes continued to plead with her long after he had finished speaking.

Emily stared at him and shook her head. She wanted to say yes, to take the chance, more than she had ever wanted anything in her life. But her mother's story was just one example of how things went terribly wrong for those who followed their hearts. "I'm sorry, Mr. Ball, but I cannot risk it."

CHAPTER 18

November 20, 1889, Iron Creek, Minnesota

It seemed to Richard that the entire town had turned out to see the production of Shakespeare's *As You Like It.* As the curtain went down, the entire theater erupted in rapturous applause. "Who would have thought a place like Iron Creek would have this little treasure?" Aunt Mary said, her eyes alight with pleasure.

"It is certainly unexpected," Richard agreed. The cast emerged onto the stage once more for a curtain call, and many people got to their feet. A few whistled their pleasure. "It is such a shame that Miss Watson could not be here to see it with us."

"The play, or that everyone in town is here, all mixing together?" Aunt Mary asked as she slipped an arm through his. "She has her reasons for feeling that way. You have to respect that."

"Her reason is Boston-based. It has nothing to do with a life here," Richard said angrily.

"My dear, she needs time to think. You came out here so suddenly. How else was she to react? She has learned so much and has even more to come to terms with. It was clumsy and foolish of you to add to that."

"Thank you for your support," he said drily. But he knew she was right. He had blundered in, with no consideration of all she had gone through, only thinking of his own happiness.

Aunt Mary raised her head and tutted at him. Then, seeing that the rest of their row had already begun to leave the theater, she nudged him hard in the ribs. "We can talk about this more later. Tonight is for fun and laughter with our new friends."

They made their way out into the foyer, where a few familiar faces were milling around, glasses in their hands, chatting. Aunt Mary joined Mrs. Cable and Nelly Graham, and Richard spotted Geoffrey Drayton and his wife, Jeannie. He waved and went to join them.

"How is the Ford house coming along?" Richard asked, not really interested but wanting to get an idea of when Geoffrey would be free to work on his house.

Geoffrey saw right through him. "I shall be starting work for you in ten days," he promised. He turned to his wife and smiled at her. "Mr. Ball will finally be making the old Bailey place a home again."

"Oh, I am glad," Mrs. Drayton said, beaming at Richard. "Every child growing up here in the past twenty years has played house in that place. I used to go there a lot, to get away from my many siblings, for a little peace and quiet."

"We fell in love with it as soon as we saw it," Richard said. "I cannot wait to see what your husband can do with it. I understand you built the theater, too, Geoffrey?"

"I did, even down to the seats you sit on – though the milliner in town helped me with the upholstery."

Jonny pushed through the crowd and greeted them all. "So, what did you think?" he asked eagerly.

"I loved it. Geoffrey fell asleep, as usual," Mrs. Drayton said with a grin.

"And you and your aunt?" Jonny asked Richard.

"We loved it. It is one of my aunt's favorite plays," Richard said. "It is quite a relief to her that she will not have to go without the pleasure of the theater living here."

"I only wish we could put on more productions," Jonny said wistfully. "We are reliant upon traveling companies, and few like to travel up this far. I do what I can to get them, but it would be wonderful if, one day, we could afford our own troupe."

"I think that would be wonderful," Mrs. Drayton said. "I presume it would be very expensive?"

"To get it up and running, yes, but given the audiences

we can provide, I think it would be a sound investment in the long term," Jonny said. "Perhaps it is time that I started to ask around for people who might be interested."

"You can put me down on your list," Richard said. "I'm not rich, but Uncle Edward left my aunt and me a sizable amount that we would very much like to put to good use. Just let me know when you have something in mind."

"Good man," Jonny said, slapping Richard on the back. "Now, I must go and find my wife."

Richard chatted with the Draytons for a little longer, then went to fetch his aunt. She looked a little tired, so he wanted to get her back to the rooms above the law office before she wore herself out. He wrapped her up in her coat and covered her with fur blankets before getting up on the driver's bench of their newly purchased gig.

"I am so glad we moved here," she said happily, looking up at the stars in the sky. "The air is so fresh. Even though everything is covered in snow and it is so cold you could freeze to death if you stayed out too long, it is perfect, isn't it?"

"It is," Richard agreed, keeping his eyes on the track. Jonny had men keeping it clear of snow, but there were often icy patches that were hard to see. Mabel, their sure-footed pony, had been recommended to them by Alec Jenks, the local blacksmith in charge of the public stables. Richard had never been so glad to place his trust in the big man. Mabel was far more adept at dealing with the icy conditions than he was.

"Do you think Miss Watson will come back to visit her father?"

"No, Aunt. I think he will go to her. She would never be able to afford the fare, and she would never accept the money from Mayor Winston. Or anyone else."

"Pride is sometimes a terrible thing," Aunt Mary said sleepily. "It can make you miss out on so many of life's real blessings."

Richard couldn't help agreeing with her, but there was little he could do about it for the time being. He had not given up on Miss Emily Watson, though. He loved her. She had admitted that she had feelings for him, too. So, he would wait and give her the time she needed. He would write to her every week, just telling her of his time in Iron Creek, and he would visit her in Boston from time to time. In the end, she would see that things need not be as they had been for her mother and father.

DECEMBER 3, 1889, Boston, Massachusetts

"There's a letter for you on the table," Marta called from upstairs as Emily came in from work. "It's from him." She ran down the stairs and watched as Emily picked up the letter and opened it slowly.

"No," Emily said, throwing it back onto the table. "I don't want to hear what he has to say. It is better for us both if we just forget the past months ever happened."

Marta picked up the letter and began to read it. She sighed, and a strange look crossed her face as she sat down at the kitchen table. "Oh, Em," she said. "I really don't know why on earth you are still here when that beautiful man is there waiting for you."

"He is not waiting for me," Emily said, snatching the letter from Marta's hands.

"Oh, he definitely is," Marta teased as Emily began to read his words.

Dear Miss Watson

I know we did not part on the terms that perhaps either of us might have wished for, but I need you to know that this is not done. We are not done. I told you that I love you. I meant it, and I have never said that to anyone else before. I hope I will never need to say it to anyone else in the future – for I am not giving up on you. On us.

I did not respond to your letter, thinking that I might perhaps find a bride. As you know, my uncle placed that advertisement just before he died. I had no desire to wed when we met. But everything changed when we did. Your hopes and dreams suddenly became mine, and finding your father became the most important thing in the world to me because I hoped it would answer the questions you needed answering and might bring you the peace and happiness you deserve.

As time went on, you became the person I wanted to run to with all manner of news, trivial and of consequence. I wanted to hear what you thought about things – and to see your beautiful face. I have never seen eyes quite like yours, so blue they are almost violet.

My offer of marriage still stands. But I understand that perhaps you need time to be sure that I mean it and that I am truly the only man for you. I may not be poor, and I did not grow up scrimping and scraping for every bite to eat, but I can assure you that I did not grow up thinking any man or woman is inherently better or worse than any other man or woman on account of their birth and social standing. My aunt would be appalled that she raised me so poorly if I had turned out to be that manner of man.

So, we are going to do what people normally do when they become acquainted via the matrimonials advertisements. We are going to write to each other. And you will write to me because you do love me. And if you do not write, I shall return to Boston and demand to know why.

Yours with all my heart

Richard Ball

"If I were you, I would already be halfway to the railway station." Marta sighed dreamily. "I do not think I will ever understand why you are still here and not there. Even if he hadn't asked you to marry him, you have a chance of a different life, a better life, with him and with your father."

"But what if everyone thinks I am only in love with his money?" Emily asked, tears pouring down her cheeks. "What if he realizes, once he knows me better, that he cannot bear the way I slurp my soup or the way I talk?"

"Oh, Em, I know that your father's family made your mother feel like she wasn't good enough for them, but the truth is that they weren't good enough for her. You know that, don't you?"

Emily nodded. "I just…" She tailed off, unsure of what she had been about to say.

"You don't need to marry him straight away, but you could at least allow him to court you."

"Would you truly give up everything here if you were in my place?"

"Emily Watson, I'll come with you if it proves that to you," Marta said with a grin. "I'd not say no to a better life than this."

"There's a bakery there. It is incredible. If you could get a job there, you would learn so much," Emily said.

"Then let's go," Marta said. "I mean, what is there to stop us? I don't have a family, and your family is there. I know you'll miss Harriet and her family, but she'll want what is best for you. The only thing either of us has to lose is our jobs, and you've just told me that there may be an even better one for me there, and you hate yours."

"I do, but there is no mill in Iron Creek. What else could I do?"

"Anything. You're clever, you learn fast, and are never late. There's bound to be something you can do there."

Emily stared at the letter again, then looked at Marta. She was right. There was nothing to keep them in Boston other than the security of the known. Perhaps it was time she took a chance for something better. But something was nagging at her still. "How will we pay our fare?"

Marta laughed. "That is the least of our worries. Just send a telegram to your father, I'm sure he'll be glad to send us the tickets."

"I couldn't."

"Oh yes, you can," Marta insisted. "If we are doing this, we need to do it quickly, before you change your mind and talk us both out of it. I will give notice to Mr. White tomorrow. Did you hear, he and Mrs. Jarnley are getting married? I doubt he'll care if we leave tomorrow, he's so happy."

"I am pleased for them," Emily said. "He's been sweet on her for the longest time."

Marta fetched a bottle of beer from the kitchen with two small glasses. "It's not champagne," she said as she opened the bottle and poured it out, "but I think we should toast to our new life in Minnesota. May we both be happier there than we've ever been here."

"I will drink to that," Emily said. They clinked their

glasses together and drank. She had never felt more excited, or more afraid, in her entire life.

CHAPTER 19

December 8, 1889, On the Train

Having received Emily's telegram, Mayor Winston wasted no time in arranging for her to draw the funds required to purchase tickets for her and Marta's travel from a lawyers' office in Boston. It had been unbelievably simple. All of Emily's worries that it might be too much trouble or take weeks for him to send the tickets to them were clearly unfounded. *How different life is for the wealthy* she had thought as she had signed the document in Mr. Bedford's office, and he had handed her the funds.

It was as well that everything had been arranged so swiftly. Had it taken any longer, Emily was sure that she would have changed her mind and not gone through with it. To move hundreds of miles north in the middle of winter – when Minnesota would be shrouded in thick snow and ice –

seemed foolhardy in the extreme. She had warned Marta what they could expect, but she was sure that her friend did not quite believe that the winter cold could be any worse than that in Boston.

Even now, sitting in a first-class compartment and staring at the world passing by the window, Emily couldn't help thinking that she had made a terrible mistake. Marta, who was usually so level-headed, had become positively giddy since she had learned of Mr. Ball's unexpected proposal. She seemed to think that Iron Creek was the answer to all the miseries in life. Emily had tried to convince her that she wasn't sure if she wanted to marry Mr. Ball. After all, they barely knew each other. No, for her, this trip was about getting to know both of the new men in her life, nothing more.

"Have you told him you're coming?" Marta asked.

"My father, of course. Otherwise we'd not be sitting in this compartment," Emily said. She knew who Marta meant, but she wasn't in the mood for another dreamy retelling of all Mr. Ball's finest features.

"You know full well that I meant Mr. Ball," Marta said. "I do not understand your reticence toward him. He is the most marriageable man either of us is ever likely to meet, and he likes you. No, he loves you."

"How can he possibly love me, Marta?" Emily asked. "He barely knows me. He's seen no more than a snapshot of who I am. I am always on my very best behavior when I am around him. I speak more carefully, choosing my words and trying not to let him hear the woman who works in a mill."

"You speak beautifully," Marta said, frowning at her. "The idea that you have to speak differently with him is silly, and you know it. I've not noticed you acting differently around him. I think he knows you as well as any of us do. In many ways, he may know you better. You told him things so he might find your father that you had not told me."

"I had to tell him those things," Emily protested. "I certainly did not tell him because he was a close confidante. I told him because I had to because he was acting on my behalf."

Marta did not look convinced, but Emily knew that she had not shared anything with Mr. Ball that she would not have shared with any attorney – except perhaps that chilly picnic down by the creek. That had most certainly not been a professional encounter, but it was one that she revisited often in her dreams. She was fond of Mr. Ball, of course she was, and it would be easy to accept his proposal. But it was all too sudden and too strange. She had so many things that she needed to learn about herself, her father, and him before she could accept it.

"I could not have said no," Marta admitted. "I cannot imagine a man like him even looking at a girl like me."

"And neither can I, which is why I had to say no," Emily said. "Despite what anyone says about this country being a place of opportunity, it is also still a place of strict social boundaries. I need him to be sure that he is ready to face what that would bring. I need to know that I can face a lifetime of his kind whispering behind my back, claiming that I somehow cast a spell over him, measuring my waist with their eyes on our wedding day, sure that he would only be marrying me because he had put a child in my belly. There will always be those that will presume that I only want him for his money and position, and I don't know if either of us is truly ready for that."

"But you don't want those things. If anyone in the world has no desire for such things, it is you, Em. You're the only person I know who is truly happy with her lot, though I know you would have changed your job in a heartbeat if you could!"

"I know that. You know that. I believe Mr. Ball knows that, or he would not have asked me to marry him. But there will be others who do not. I am not sure I want to be faced with that every time we step out in public."

Marta sighed. "I had not thought of all of that," she said sadly. "It is a terrible world that we live in, where people are judged by those who have no business doing so. Mr. Ball doesn't strike me as the kind of man who gives a fig for such nonsense."

"I don't think he does, and his aunt seems very kind, too. But they are not the only people in their world, even if he believes Iron Creek to be different."

"That is certainly true," Marta agreed. "But you are of

his class now, aren't you? I mean, your father is the mayor. He must have some wealth?"

"I believe he does, and his house is certainly the finest in Iron Creek. But no matter who he is or what he has, I am my mother's daughter. I grew up in her world, not his."

Marta could think of nothing more to say, and they both fell quiet for some time. When her friend's stomach began to growl, Emily took her to the restaurant car, where they had a good lunch. Feeling full and lulled by the movement of the train, they both fell asleep. Emily woke up to find the world outside had gone dark, not that it mattered much. They had a long journey ahead, and Chicago was the end of the line.

She couldn't deny to herself, though she might do to Marta, that Mr. Ball was a large part of the reason she had let Marta talk her into this crazy flit across the country. She did like him. Too much, if she was completely honest. And she wanted to believe that Iron Creek was different. Her experience there had shown her that the people were friendly enough, but she had been there for such a short time. It was hard to know if such kindness would continue.

What would she do if it did not? If the people could not accept her? Just because she was the mayor's daughter, that did not grant her immediate acceptance. And what was she going to do with her time once she got there? She did not want to rely on her father's charity. She was used to working hard to earn her way. But with no mills, she could think of little that she was qualified to do. She was too old to be taken on as an apprentice, after all.

There were still so many questions. She had truly thought that the questions would stop once she knew who her father was, but somehow there seemed to be even more of them flying around in her head now. She wondered what her mother would think of what she and Marta were doing. Mom would always have wanted her to be happy, but Emily was sure that she would have counseled against falling in love with a man like Mr. Ball, especially after her own experiences. Of course, Mom would have wanted her to know her father. If only she had known that Mayor Winston was still alive, she might still have been alive. Their lives would have been so different if they had been a family, together in Iron Creek. Perhaps Emily was heading to the place she should have been all along. Only time would tell.

DECEMBER 10, 1889, Iron Creek, Minnesota

"You're looking particularly cheerful today," Richard said. He had run into Mayor Winston on the street just outside the sheriff's office.

"Emily arrives this evening," Mayor Winston said, looking a little confused, as if Richard should somehow already know that.

"Emily is coming?"

"She is. Didn't she write to you?

"No, but she has no reason to," Richard assured the mayor. "After all, she is no longer my client. I am not her attorney now."

The mayor shrugged. "I rather thought that the two of you were friends. Perhaps something more than friends, even."

"On my part, perhaps, but your daughter made it quite clear to me that she was not interested in me," Richard said, unable to keep the bitterness from his voice. He had been smarting ever since Miss Watson had rebuffed him. She had shown no desire that night to move to Iron Creek or to be with him, so her sudden change of heart could only be because she wanted to get to know her father. But then again, there was the letter he had sent to her. Perhaps she had received it and that was why she was coming here, now? But surely, if that were the case, she would have sent him word of her imminent arrival? Oh, nothing made any sense anymore.

"I am sorry to hear that," Mayor Winston said comfortingly. "I would have been happy to have you call upon her."

"I am glad that she has decided to come here to spend some time with you. How long will she be staying?"

"I think her intention is forever. She's given up her job, and her friend is coming with her. Wesley is very keen to speak with her after I told him she works in the best bakery in Boston."

"She does. Her pastries are almost as good as Mr. Baker's," Richard said, remembering them fondly. He was glad that Emily would have company on the long journey, but Marta's presence told him even more strongly than anything else could that Emily was not coming to be a wife. The two of them were coming to start a new life. He felt his heart break all over again.

He went about his day, following up on several new cases that the townsfolk had brought to him. He found his mind wandering, constantly trying to decipher what the news of Emily's arrival could mean. He started to make silly mistakes and there were balls of crumpled paper all around his feet because he was so distracted. None of the cases were difficult matters to resolve. Most of them were to do with boundary disputes between neighbors, but there were a few more complex matters that meant he would need to visit the law library at the university in Minneapolis. Deciding that it was as good a day as any to make that trip, under the circumstances as he seemed to be unable to concentrate on anything long enough to get the work done, he hurried to his office and finished up the matters that needed his attention, and then went upstairs to pack.

"I thought you weren't going to Minneapolis until next week," Aunt Mary said, coming in from her now regular lunch with Mrs. Cable and Nelly Graham. She took off her hat and the thick fur coat that Richard had purchased from

Old Porter for her to keep out the cold and placed them on the stand by the door.

"I wasn't, but I decided that I'd rather not put it off any longer," Richard said a little evasively.

"That choice has nothing to do with the gossip in town that Miss Watson is returning to Iron Creek, does it?"

"And, what if it does?"

"Richard, it is none of my business how you deal with matters in your life, but you cannot run from her forever. Nelly told me that she will be staying for good. You will have to learn how to be with her, and sooner rather than later."

"I know." Richard sighed. "I am being a coward, but I simply cannot face her yet. I was a fool. I took a risk and followed my heart, and she rightly turned me down. And then I wrote and made an even bigger fool of myself. I just don't think I am ready to see the pity in her eyes just yet."

"I doubt she will pity you," Aunt Mary said, shaking her head. "She's far too sensible for that. And I doubt that she would be coming here if she was entirely indifferent to you."

"She's coming to see her father."

"That is what she has said and the reason she has given to him and would no doubt give to anyone else, including you. But her father could have visited her in Boston. They were both quite reconciled to the idea of writing to each other and him visiting her there. No, I'd say that her change of heart has more to do with you than with him. Because the timing is peculiarly linked to when your letter would have reached Boston."

"Do not get my hopes up, Aunt Mary. It isn't fair to tease a man that way," Richard pleaded.

"My darling boy, you are a fine attorney and a good man. Why not use your attorney's head on this one rather than that of a good man? A young woman gives up everything she has worked for, everything she knows, to travel to the snowy wastes of Minnesota, not long after a rather handsome, and eligible, young man proposes marriage to her, and insists in a letter that his proposal stands? If you cannot see it, then I despair of you."

Richard did not stop packing, but his aunt's words echoed in his head as he made his way to the railway station to get the train to Minneapolis. A large, red locomotive pulled up at the platform as he arrived. Several people got off it, crowding the platform and hurrying to get out of the station. Richard saw Mayor Winston standing at the very platform edge, looking up and down the carriages anxiously. Two young women approached him, and he beamed as one threw her arms around him. Richard knew that she would be Miss Watson and the other young woman was Miss Pauling.

Richard felt a peculiar mixture of delight that he had brought father and daughter together and abject misery that she did not want him. He could feel tears pricking at the back of his eyes and closed them for a few moments to hold them back. He quickly paid for his ticket and ducked into the waiting room, from where he watched them leave the station through the glass door. He hated himself for being such a coward, but he had been right to take this trip. Just seeing her face again had been too much. She was so lovely to look upon, and he was not sure he would ever be able to accept that she was not to be his.

He had to accept that she had turned him down. He had to respect her wishes, but Aunt Mary might have a point. The timing was uncanny. His letter must have reached Boston not long before Miss Watson set out on her journey. It seemed unlikely that she had not received it. And here she was, having given up everything she had ever known. He did not dare let himself hope that she was there for him, though every inch of him prayed that she was.

CHAPTER 20

December 13, 1889, Iron Creek, Minnesota

It was hard for Emily not to react to Marta's delight as the two women explored Iron Creek together. Despite the ice and snow and the freezing temperatures, Marta was totally enamored with the little town. Emily had to admit that she was rather enjoying being back, too. Her father was delighted that she had reconsidered, and he had hardly stopped smiling since they'd arrived. But she had not yet seen Mr. Ball. Apparently, he was out of town on business. Emily couldn't help feeling a little sad about that. She also felt a little nervous, not knowing exactly when she would see him. She had done all she could to prepare herself during the journey, but now that had to wait.

"Can we visit the bakery again?" Marta asked eagerly. She had already had a very successful meeting with Mr.

Baker, who was delighted to find someone with as much passion for baking as himself and had hired her on the spot. "I want to get some more of that *clafoutis*. I've never tasted anything so delicious. He tells me it is very simple to make, very typical French country fare, but it is exquisite."

"I do hope so, though I wonder where he gets the cherries from at this time of year," Emily agreed.

"Oh, he dries them in summer, then soaks them in brandy for three days before they go into the dessert," Marta gushed. "I asked him."

"No wonder I slept so well the other night, then," Emily said with a grin.

They walked arm in arm toward the bakery. Emily's eyes darted left and right, always looking for Mr. Ball. She knew he wasn't back, but she couldn't help herself. She so longed to see him, yet she also dreaded it. It was a peculiar state to find herself in, and she wished he would hurry up and get back so that they could sort matters out between them. She had to know if he had truly meant everything he had said and everything he had written in his letter. She still wasn't sure if she was ready to marry him, but she needed to know it was real before she could make up her mind.

She did not doubt that she cared for him, that she loved him. He was possibly the most handsome man she had ever known. And he was charming, polite, and good. He made her laugh, and he was generous. Quite simply, there was nothing about him to dislike. Her only concern was still the one that had caused her own mother and father so much pain. She had to be sure that such judgments would not come their way, that there would be no shame for him or misery for her if they took that ultimate step.

The bakery was warm and smelled delicious. Marta immediately began to quiz the poor woman behind the counter about what ingredients Mr. Baker had used to create all the delicious-looking treats available that day. In desperation, the woman called for him.

"Ah, Miss Pauling," he said with a grin. "Might I introduce the two of you? Clarice, this is my new assistant baker, Marta Pauling. Miss Pauling, this is my wife. Please be kind to her."

Marta flushed beet red. "I am sorry, Mrs. Baker. I would have been more respectful if I had known."

"No matter," Mrs. Baker said with a grin. "I am glad Wesley has found someone as obsessed as himself."

"I suppose that I should have known who was here when Clarice said there was someone in the shop wanting to know all my secrets," Mr. Baker said. "Can you not wait until Monday? I promise I will teach you all I know then."

Marta chuckled. "I suppose so. I shall enjoy the mystery and try to guess the ingredients of the items I eat in the meantime," she said. "Do you have any *clafoutis* today? We enjoyed it so much the night we arrived."

"Sadly, no, I am sold out," Mr. Baker said. "But I can assure you that my cherry pie is almost as delicious."

“Then we shall take a cherry pie,” Marta said happily.

“I will see you at four o’clock on Monday. Don’t be late.”

“Four o’clock will be a late start for me,” she said. “I had to be in by half past three in Boston.”

The girls walked back to Mayor Winston’s grand house and let themselves in. The mayor wasn’t home, and the house was unusually quiet. Marta made her way straight to the kitchen, where she began to pull out the ingredients for the supper she had planned. Emily sank down in a chair at the large kitchen table and put her head in her hands.

“Are you unhappy?” Marta asked. “Do you regret coming here?”

“No. At least, I don’t think I do,” Emily said wearily. “I suppose I am just tired of waiting for him to come back so we can talk. There is so much that needs to be said.”

“What if he doesn’t want to talk? Will you regret coming here then?”

“How could I?” Emily asked. “You have the job of your dreams ahead of you, and my father is so happy to have me here.”

“Forget us,” Marta told her. “What about you? You put everyone and everything else ahead of your own happiness all the time. You could have said yes to Mr. Ball when he asked before he left Boston, but you were worried about what his friends and acquaintances would say. You could have sent him a telegram telling him we were coming here because you love him, but you didn't. Was it because you didn't want to get his hopes up?"

"Honestly, I don't know," Emily admitted. "I still have concerns." She paused, trying to find the right words, then sighed heavily. "I don't want what happened to my parents to happen to us."

"How could it? His aunt likes you. Your father likes him. Nobody is looking to split you apart but you, Em?"

"I know," Emily said sadly. "I know. I am just too afraid to trust that everything will work out well."

Marta gave her a quick hug, then returned to chopping the vegetables. "At some point, you are going to have to let go and take that leap, Em. And we'll all be here for you if it works out, or if it doesn't."

RICHARD WAS on the train home. He hadn't found everything he needed, but he knew that he couldn't stay any longer. He had to get back to Iron Creek. He needed to talk with Miss Watson and let her know he would wait however long it might take. He would prove to her that his love was constant and do whatever he needed to do to prove to her that nobody in Iron Creek would stand in the way of their happiness. Given what had happened to her parents before she was even born, he could understand her reticence, but Iron Creek was not Boston, nor was it Philadelphia.

Aunt Mary was probably right, as she invariably was. The timing of Miss Watson's coming to Iron Creek could only have been influenced by his letter. That she had not told him she was coming could have been an oversight, or perhaps she had feared she might not be able to say what she needed to on paper and wanted to see him in person. If her answer had been no, she would have written to him and told him so. She would not have wanted him to return to Boston to beg her, so not writing would not have been an option.

Instead, she had traveled to Minnesota. If she did not wish to speak with him, why travel to the very town that he had made his home? Even if she was not yet ready to accept his proposal, he could at least court her and show her that Iron Creek would not judge them the way Boston would have done. Her being there meant there truly was hope, and he would cling to it with all his might.

It was dark when he got off the train, and too late to call on anyone. He walked along Main Street, past the saloon and Mayor Winston's house, where he stopped and looked up at it for a few moments, wondering which room was Miss Watson's, and then carried on walking. The lights in the law office were on. He frowned. Nobody should have been in there while he was gone. After all, he had not yet found a suitable secretary.

Cautiously, he went to unlock the door and was surprised to find it unlocked. He went inside and quietly locked it behind him. If someone had broken in, it was the only way out, and locking it would slow their passage. There was nobody in the outer office, where he hoped there might one day be a secretary's desk. He switched off the lights behind him as he made his way to his office in the back. There was light on there, as well. He slowly pushed the door open and felt a little foolish when he found nobody there either. Aunt Mary must have forgotten to lock the door and turn out the lamps as she passed through.

He turned them all out now and made his way up the stairs. It was unusually quiet, and there was no sign of Aunt Mary. Everything was very peculiar. He looked in the small kitchen and their cozy parlor, then knocked on Aunt Mary's door. There was no reply. She hadn't said anything about an engagement, and he could not imagine her going out and leaving everything alight and unlocked. He decided to peek around the door. The room was dark, but he could make out a lump on the floor that should not be there. He quickly fetched a lamp from the parlor and entered the room.

Aunt Mary was lying on the floor, her breathing slow and labored and her skin as white as the sheets she had dragged from the bed as she fell. "Aunt Mary, stay right there," Richard told her. He knelt beside her and pressed a kiss to her forehead, then quickly felt for her pulse. It was faint and a little erratic. "I am going to fetch the doctor. Don't you dare give up breathing while I am gone."

He ran back along Main Street to the medical clinic. There was usually someone there at all hours. If there wasn't, Dr. Anna lived just a few doors along, and Dr. Lancelot and his wife lived in the rooms above. Richard banged on the locked door loudly. "Doctor, help, it's an emergency. My aunt is very sick."

Nelly Graham opened the door. "Whatever has happened to Mary?" she asked, reaching for a black medical bag. "Dr. Lancelot is in Duluth tonight, so we'll stop for Dr. Anna on the way."

She stopped at the doctor's house and banged the door loudly. Dr. Anna soon emerged, wrapped in a heavy fur coat. Alec, her husband, was not far behind her.

"She's barely breathing, and her pulse is weak," Richard explained as they hurried back to Aunt Mary's side. They all trooped up the stairs to the rooms. "Through there," Richard said, pointing to Aunt Mary's door. "When I came back, every light was on, the door downstairs unlocked, and I found her here."

They both knelt beside her. Nelly stayed close by, her face full of fear for her friend. Alec could be heard in the kitchen, pouring water into the kettle in case hot water was needed or to make a cup of tea, Richard had no idea which. He didn't care, as long as Dr. Anna could save Aunt Mary. As the doctor carefully examined her patient, Richard paced nervously.

"I need to take her to the clinic. There are things I can do for her there that I can't here. Tell Alec he's needed."

Nelly went to get him when it was clear that Richard was

not going to leave his aunt's side. The big blacksmith appeared and picked up Aunt Mary as if she were as light as a feather. They all went back to the clinic, and Aunt Mary was soon settled into a comfortable bed.

"We'll soon have her well again," Nelly assured Richard. "I'll stay by her side every moment."

"No, you won't," Dr. Anna admonished her, "or you'll end up sick, too, Nelly. You've been at the clinic since five o'clock this morning as it is. No, you'll go home to bed. I'll stay with her tonight, and Dr. Lancelot will take over in the morning. Richard, there is a bed there," she said, pointing to the bed beside his aunt's. "If you want to stay here, you can, but you must promise to let us do our jobs and not get in the way."

"I promise," Richard assured her. "Just make her well."

CHAPTER 21

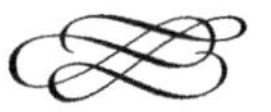

December 14, 1889, Iron Creek, Minnesota

The news that Mrs. Ball had taken ill in the night was all around the town the next morning. Emily knew that Mr. Ball must be beside himself with worry. He adored his aunt. Not even thinking about the awkwardness between them, she hurried to the clinic. She had to know if there was anything she could do to help. It was the very least she owed him after all he had done for her, and the least she owed Mrs. Ball. Emily had tried to return the coat and boots the older woman had so kindly lent her, but Mrs. Ball had refused and insisted they were a gift.

The clinic was quiet. As the bell of the door clanged to announce her arrival, Dr. Lancelot appeared. He was an elderly gentleman with a kind face, and Emily decided she liked him straight away. He smiled at her. "Can I help?"

"I am rather hoping that I might be of assistance to you. Or, rather, to Mrs. Ball," she said. "I understand she's not well, and she has been so kind to me."

"I shall fetch her nephew," Dr. Lancelot said kindly. "If he cannot think of anything useful for you to do, I am sure I can find something as Dr. Anna sent Nelly home for a much-needed rest."

Mr. Ball emerged a few moments later. He looked wrung out. Emily wished she could wrap her arms around him and soothe his worries. Instead, she stood in front of him, feeling terribly awkward. "How is she?" she asked when he didn't seem to have anything to say.

"Better than she was when I found her, but both doctors seem concerned still," he said. "I should never have left. Heaven only knows how long she was lying there, waiting for someone to come and help her."

"You must not blame yourself," Emily said immediately. "Such things can happen at any time."

"Ah, but I would have been here if I hadn't been a fool, trying to avoid speaking to you."

Emily stared at him. Of all the things he might have said to her, she hadn't expected that. "You didn't want to speak to me? You didn't want me to come here?"

"Oh, Emily, of course I wanted you to come here, and I've wanted to do nothing but speak to you ever since we parted," he said, sounding tired and exasperated all at once. "But I wasn't ready because you hadn't warned me you were coming. Your father told me on the day you were to arrive, and I panicked."

"But why?"

"Because I thought you could not possibly have come here for me, and I feared that I had made a terrible fool of myself. I wish I had stayed, even if you had told me that you never wished to see me again. If I had, then perhaps Aunt Mary would still be well."

Dr. Lancelot must have overheard them, for he hurried toward Mr. Ball, shaking his head. "No, you must not let yourself think that way," he said firmly, taking Mr. Ball's arms and looking him straight in the eye. "What happened to your aunt could have happened at any time. There is nothing you, nor I, nor Dr. Anna could have done to stop it. Apoplexy is a mysterious thing, and it seems to come out of nowhere. But we are lucky. It could have been much worse. I think there is a very good hope that your aunt will make a good recovery, if not a full one. Please stop blaming yourself, Richard. It does nobody any good."

Emily nodded her agreement. "You have to be strong for her, Mr. Ball," she said. "And we have all the time in the world to discuss everything else. For now, we must look after her. From the look of you, you've not slept a wink all night. Go home, have a nap and a wash, and come back this afternoon."

"I'll not leave her," he protested.

"You must be well and strong to assist her," Dr. Lancelot said, agreeing with Emily's prescription.

"I promise I will stay here with her and will run for you if anything changes, for better or worse," Emily said. "I'll not leave her side otherwise."

Reluctantly, Mr. Ball allowed them to send him home. Emily took up the seat beside Mrs. Ball, but within moments, she felt guilty for just sitting there, doing nothing. She popped her head around Dr. Lancelot's office door. "Is there anything I can do, while I wait?" she asked.

He smiled at her. "Nelly has a list of all the things that need doing around here. I'm sure there will be something on there that you can do." He went out into the reception area and rummaged in the drawers under Nelly's desk. "Aha," he crowed, waving a piece of paper at her as he stood back up.

Emily took the list and smiled. "I think there are some things on this list that I can get on with while keeping my promise to stay with Mrs. Ball."

When Mr. Ball returned, he found her mending the sheets while chatting away with his aunt. "How are you feeling?" he asked, bending down to press a kiss on the older woman's forehead.

She blinked a couple of times and tried to smile, but the left side of her mouth refused to move. "We think that it means she is happy when she blinks. Or it means yes," Emily explained. "One blink is for no or if she's feeling bad."

"It's the same system we used when I was little." Richard exclaimed. "I used to lose my voice all the time with such a sore throat. She used to make me rest my voice until the pain was gone." Mrs. Ball blinked twice again, confirming he was right. "I hope Miss Watson has taken good care of you." Two blinks, a pause, then a further two blinks.

"Thank you, Mrs. Ball. I've done little but talk and sing, I'm glad you haven't minded me talking nonsense to you." Another two blinks. Emily smiled at her, picked up her pile of mending, and turned to leave the room.

"Thank you, Miss Watson, I cannot thank you enough," Mr. Ball said.

"I'm happy to come whenever you cannot," she said simply. "I've nothing else to do, and I like it here."

She put the mending away in a cupboard and went to say goodbye to Dr. Lancelot. He was in a meeting with Dr. Anna. "I just wanted to let you know I'm leaving. The mended sheets are in the cupboard."

"No, wait," Dr. Anna said with a smile. "Come in. As a matter of fact, we were just talking about you. The clinic keeps growing, and Andrew and myself are agreed that we really do need another nurse. Nelly isn't as young as she was, though she'd never let us say anything about slowing down, and you've been such a help this morning. Would you be interested in joining us?"

Emily was taken aback. She hadn't expected anything like this. "But I have no experience."

"Nelly would be the first to tell you that a good nurse learns as she goes. The most important thing is that she has a good heart. All of us know you have that," Dr. Lancelot said kindly. "After all, the first thing you did when you heard about Mrs. Ball was rush here to see what you could do to help."

"I suppose I did."

"The hours are terrible, and the work is often hard, smelly, and dirty, but it is rewarding in so many ways," Dr. Anna said.

"You've convinced me," Emily said with a nervous laugh. "I'll do it."

The bell over the door clanged, announcing someone's arrival. Dr. Anna went to see who it was. Emily smiled at Dr. Lancelot. "Thank you," she said. "I'll not let you down."

"I know you won't. The only person I've ever known get through that much of Nelly's list in such a short time is Nelly herself."

Emily bumped into Dr. Anna in the corridor. "Miss Emily Watson, this is Mrs. Bronwen Gustavson. She also helps us out here from time to time."

"I'm more of an assistant to Nelly than anything else," Mrs. Gustavson said, smiling at Emily. "I mostly help Andrew with his correspondence so Nelly can do all the nursing. With my family, coming here is a respite."

"Bronwen has twins, and another one on the way," Dr. Anna said with a grin, pointing at Bronwen's round belly.

"I'm pleased to meet you," Emily said with a smile. "I'm not sure how much help I will be, but I will do my best."

"Go home now. Nelly is in tomorrow morning," Dr. Anna said. "I think it would be best if you train with her. I'll stop by and tell her on my way out to the house calls in a moment."

"Thank you again," Emily said. "I'll just check on Mrs. Ball before I go."

"See, already cares for her patients," Dr. Anna said. She and Bronwen laughed.

Emily said her goodbyes. As she walked back home, she couldn't help thinking about the way Dr. Anna, Dr. Lancelot, and Mrs. Gustavson had acted with one another. In Boston, the idea of calling a doctor by their first name was unheard of. Everyone in the clinic using first names felt utterly peculiar, as if there were no hierarchy at all. Perhaps Richard had been right when he'd said that things were different here.

As she passed the bakery, Marta was coming out, having purchased something delicious for supper. "He's going to be sick of you before you even start work," Emily joked.

"No, he loves that I care about it as much as he does," Marta said happily.

"Does his wife not mind you monopolizing his time?"

"No. Clarice is wonderful," Marta said. "She's glad to

have him talk to me about it all so she doesn't have to listen to it."

"You call her Clarice already?" Emily marveled.

"Yes, and I am to call him Wes," Marta said. "And virtually nobody here seems to use titles or surnames. I like that everyone is the same, each respected for their individual skills and what they bring to the town."

"I have noticed the same thing," Emily said. "I was just at the clinic, and everyone there does the same thing."

"Oh, I should have asked that first. How is Mrs. Ball?" Marta looked mortified that she had forgotten something so important.

"She is doing as well as can be expected. The doctors agree that she must have had an apoplectic fit. The poor lady can't move the left side of her face or body at the moment, but she seems to be in good spirits. Much better than you'd expect, really."

"I do hope she recovers. She is such a nice old lady."

"Yes, she is. Poor Mr. Ball is in pieces. He looked dreadful when I arrived, and not much better when he came back after supposedly having some rest. I doubt he's slept a wink since it happened."

The two women let themselves into the house. The mayor was sitting in his armchair in the snug, smoking a pipe. "Oh, good day to you girls," he said. "Come in and warm yourselves by the fire. The wind is biting today. It's given you both a bit of color in your cheeks."

"I must politely decline," Marta said. "I need to take these to the kitchen and help your cook make lunch."

Emily gave her an odd look, then realized that her friend was trying to give father and daughter some time alone. She smiled at Marta and went into the snug with her father. He sat down in his armchair and relit his pipe, and she took the sofa opposite.

"How is Mrs. Ball?" her father asked.

"As well as can be expected," Emily said. "They think it is apoplexy."

"Poor woman. And poor Richard."

"Yes, indeed," Emily said.

"Emily," Logan said softly, "there is something I should tell you now. I don't want it to be something that is hidden between us. This house…" He paused for a moment, then exhaled sharply. "This house does not belong to me."

"It doesn't?" Emily asked, not entirely sure why he was telling her that.

"No. I paid for it and furnished it, then I gave it to the town, to be the dwelling place of its mayors, present and future."

"Oh. That is most generous of you."

"Not really. The money was my share of my father's will. He never bothered to have me written out of it, though he threatened it often enough. I said from the start that I did not want his money. I came here for a new start, and everything I have made of myself since then is from my own hard work. I wanted you to know that I couldn't bear to accept their money after what they did to us, not that I even knew you existed at the time. But I always knew that your mother's death was their fault, somehow."

"It was not," Emily said. "She just got sick."

"Perhaps, but I did not know that then, either. Besides, had my parents not done what they did, she might have lived better and been stronger so the influenza might not have taken her from us both."

"I must confess to having wondered that, too," Emily admitted.

They sat in companionable silence for a few minutes, both lost in their memories. Emily thought of the way her mother had stroked her forehead and hair when she was sick, singing a lullaby to help her sleep when they couldn't afford to get medicine or call out a doctor. She wondered what he was thinking of but would never dare to ask.

"You don't mind that I am not as rich as I might have seemed?" he asked suddenly.

"Not at all," Emily said. "In fact, it is a bit of a relief. Money makes me uncomfortable. It makes people do strange things."

"I can do nothing but agree with you there," he said softly.

CHAPTER 22

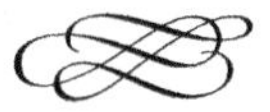

December 18, 1889, Iron Creek, Minnesota

Aunt Mary was doing well. Richard could already see a reduction in the amount of drooping in her mouth, and she was managing to hold herself up in the bed a little straighter. Her doctors were as pleased with how she was doing as they were concerned about how well she would recover. She still had little movement in her left side, though it was clear that she was feeling more there now; she flinched occasionally when she was lifted and turned your way if you stroked her left hand. She slept a lot, but when she was awake, they had conversations in which her blinking and tapping with her right hand told him her thoughts. He was hopeful that she would do well, given time.

When he'd gone in to see his aunt on Monday morning, he had been surprised to find Miss Watson in a nurse's pinafore, being taught how to take people's details when booking them in for an appointment. She'd explained that she would be working there now. He was pleased for her. She would make an excellent nurse, she was caring and warm but wise enough to accept that not all can be saved. It also meant that he got to see her every day.

They still had not had time to really talk, and Richard couldn't imagine that there would be a suitable time until Aunt Mary was well. He did not dare leave Main Street for fear that someone might need to call on him in a hurry if Aunt Mary took a turn for the worse, and Emily was busy when she was at work at the clinic. It would be inappropriate to talk there.

But every day that he didn't know why Miss Watson being there was hard for him. His fears had been left hanging in the wind, with no response from her on the day that Aunt Mary had her attack of apoplexy. He reassured himself that she knew how he felt. She knew how much he cared for her. It was down to her to come to him when she was ready. When he wasn't praying for his aunt, he was hoping that Miss Watson would actually come one day and want to talk.

In the meantime, he sat with his aunt during the day, did his work at night, and tried to remember to eat and drink. As his aunt grew stronger and the doctors said she might be well enough to have other visitors, Richard felt able to relax a little. Almost the entire town seemed to have been added to

Aunt Mary's visiting roster, and just the thought of that brought a tear to his eye. They had not been there for very long, but already, Aunt Mary was important to the people of this little town. If he hadn't been sure that Iron Creek was the right place for them to be, he was now.

With a little more free time on his hands, he decided to call upon Miss Watson and ask if she would like to go walking with him after church on Sunday. She wasn't home, but her father was. "Come in, come in," Mayor Winston said. "I went to call on your aunt yesterday. She was in good spirits."

"I think her army of visitors gives her great joy," Richard said.

"When I arrived, Nelly was trying to encourage her to speak some simple words. I could tell she was a little frustrated that she could not, but her efforts seemed very close to me."

"I agree. I don't think it will be much longer before she can speak again, though it infuriates her that she can't quite do it."

"Now, how can I help you, Richard?"

"To tell you the truth, I called on your daughter," he admitted. "I did not see her at the clinic, so I rather hoped she was at home."

"I'm afraid not. She's with Dr. Anna, delivering a baby somewhere, I believe."

"She's enjoying her new work?"

"Very much," Mayor Winston said. "Her mother was a caring woman, too. She has so much of dear Janet in her."

"Please could you tell her I called? I would be most grateful if I might leave a note for her," Richard said.

"Of course, my boy. I shall be sure to give it to her myself." He took Richard into his office and handed him a sheet of paper and a pen. "Ink's there, I'll leave you to it."

Richard thanked him and waited for him to leave before dipping the pen into the inkwell. He bit his lip and wondered what to say. He decided to keep it simple. After writing the note, he let himself out of the house and went back to work. He wondered what Miss Watson would think when she read it and if she would reply. And if she did, would it be what he wanted to hear?

He was just about to lock the door of the law office and head upstairs to bed when a gentle knock sounded on the glass. He peered around the blinds and saw the chilled features of young Samuel Jellicoe. "I've a note for you, Mr. Ball," he said, handing it to Richard as he opened the door.

"Thank you, Samuel," Richard said, reaching in his pocket for a coin to give the boy.

"No need, Sir, Miss Emily's already paid me to come." He gave Richard a wink, then disappeared, heading back toward his own home.

Richard locked up, turned out the lights, and went up to the rooms. He sank into a chair and carefully opened the note, remembering how much he had enjoyed the first letter

Miss Watson had ever sent him. He wondered if this one would change his life as much as that one had.

Dear Mr. Ball,

I agree with you that it is time we talked. It seems that things have rather gotten in the way a little, and it is right that our attentions have been elsewhere. I am so glad that your aunt is recovering so well, and I hope that she will soon be back home with you.

I should be delighted to walk with you on Sunday after church. Ensure you wrap up warm. Mr. Harding told me this weekend will bring a howler. I'm not sure exactly what he means by that, but I took it to mean that it will be cold and very windy. We shall have to be careful we don't blow away.

Yours most sincerely

Emily Watson

It was short, but it was the answer he had hoped for. She would meet him, even in a gale. He could hardly put into words just how much he admired her pluck and courage. She was special to him, clever, sweet, and strong. But did she care for him as he did her? And had she learned how different things were in Iron Creek from those in Boston? He prayed that she had seen enough of this very special little town to know that because only that would make her see that they were meant to be together.

DECEMBER 22, 1889, Iron Creek, Minnesota

Thankfully, the weather was fine when Emily awoke on Sunday morning. There was no sign of Mr. Harding's howler. More than grateful for that, she stretched and sat up in bed, still finding it hard to believe that she lived in a house as fine as this. Of course, everything could change if the town were to vote for someone other than her father, but that seemed unlikely. Even though almost everyone grumbled that a man who lived in such a fine house should not be so reluctant to spend money, not one of them seemed inclined to take over, and secretly everyone agreed that he was doing a fine job. She often wondered how many of the townsfolk actually knew that he had given the house to Iron Creek, that they held as much right to its title deed as he did.

Reluctantly, she slid her legs out from under the soft, warm blankets and placed her feet on the rug. She loved the feeling of it under her feet. It was such a change from the bare, cold floorboards in the little cottage she'd shared with Marta in Boston. There was a fireplace in her bedroom, and though she knew that her father would be delighted if she lit it every day, she never had, no matter how cold it was outside. She found that the heat from the fire below, and especially the vast stove in the kitchen, kept most of the house warm enough for her.

Yesterday, she had carefully pressed her best dress and hung it up outside the armoire to be sure it would not get creased again. She wanted to look her best, so she washed and pinned her hair with particular care. She pulled on the gown moments before they would be leaving for church, then hurried down the stairs to find her father and Marta both grinning knowingly as they waited for her on the stoop. "Don't tease," she said firmly.

"We're not. I think we are as excited as you are. I do so hope it goes well," Marta gushed.

"He is a fine young man," Logan said with a smile. He offered both women an arm, and they started to walk to the church. "But it might be best to wait to find out what it is that he wishes to discuss before assuming that he will say precisely whatever it is that you wish to hear."

Emily kissed him on the cheek. "I do not expect him to say what I wish to hear. In truth, he said that some time ago. I was the one to push him away."

"But you wouldn't do that now, would you?" Marta asked anxiously. "I mean, he's perfect for you. I've said it all along. I thought you were a fool to turn him down in Boston, and you'd be an even bigger fool if you did it again here."

"We don't even know if it is his intention to ask for my hand again," Emily said. "We are simply going walking."

"Well, I should like to think that Mr. Ball is enough of a gentleman to ask your father's permission before he'd ask again," Logan said with a grin. "Now that he knows you have one who cares very deeply for your happiness."

Emily glared at them both. "The two of you are incorrigible. Please, do not make this harder than it is. Poor Mr.

Ball has enough to concern him without the pair of you spreading gossip and rumor about town."

"We've not said a word to a soul," Marta said, looking a little hurt.

"We wouldn't do such a thing," Logan added, nodding. "It's hurtful you could even think such a thing."

"Oh, I don't," Emily said quickly. "I'm just terribly nervous and talking nonsense. I'm sorry." She looked at them both, pleading with her eyes that they might forgive her. She was rewarded with a smile from Marta and a squeeze of her arm by her father. She sighed. "A part of me desperately wants him to ask for my hand again, but another part wants to get on the next train to leave the station so I don't have to talk to him at all."

"I think that's quite normal," Logan said. "I often felt like that, everything contradicting itself, when I used to call on your mother. She often told me not to, that I need not fear that she did not care for me."

"She used to tell me off for it, too," Emily said. "Perhaps it is one of those traits that I inherited from you."

"Perhaps," Logan said, smiling. "But I am so glad you resemble her and not me. The world would be a dull place indeed without those beautiful eyes in it." Emily felt her cheeks and neck flush with heat at his compliment. It was similar to one that Mr. Ball had given her, and it made her feel a little peculiar to hear that she was like her mother. It was very flattering, though.

The church was full, as it was every Sunday. Emily waved to Nelly Graham and Bronwen as her father led them to the front pew, which was his, as mayor. They waved back. Bronwen was sitting next to Amy Cable, who also waved at them all cheerfully. Emily hadn't had much chance to get to know the Cables yet, though she knew that Mr. Ball was close with them. They were the reason he had come to Iron Creek in the first place. Without them, she herself might not have been there. It was thanks to Mr. Ball's visit here that they had found her father.

She couldn't see Mr. Ball anywhere, but as he was always late for everything that didn't worry her unduly. The service was lovely. Father Paul, as always, gave a poignant sermon and chose some lovely readings from the bible for this last Sunday Mass before Christmas. Both Emily and Marta had been glad to find a committed church community in Iron Creek; their faith was important to them both. Without it, they would not have met each other, and both women valued that gift from God greatly.

When the service was over, people began to make their way out of the church. Marta was chatting enthusiastically about baking with Mr. Baker, as usual, so Emily stopped to talk to a rather bored-looking Clarice.

"I never thought there could be anyone as obsessed as he is," Clarice said, giving them an indulgent smile. "If Marta had met him before me, who knows if he'd have even noticed me?"

She was joking, but Emily couldn't help wondering if there was perhaps a hint of jealousy there, nonetheless. "Nelly told me how you two met. If anything was likely to make a man consider another woman, I would have thought that it would not be a shared love of yeast."

"What can I add but that he is a forgiving man," Clarice said. "I am a lucky woman. I'd not have blamed him if he never wished to see me again after what my brothers put him through."

"Love is a funny thing, is it not?" Emily said. "I shall drag Marta away so you may enjoy your precious time together." Clarice grinned as Emily took her friend's hand and dragged her up the aisle of the church.

Once they were outside, Marta glared at her. "That was very rude of you, Em," she said pointedly.

"No, that was me making sure you do not get between a man and his wife. It is all well and good talking about baking in the kitchens and the store, but you must leave it there. Wes has a life outside of his work, and you need to have one, too."

Marta pouted but grudgingly agreed. "You're right, as usual," she said. "I forget everything but baking when I'm near him. He is just a mind of fascinating information. He said he might send me to the man who taught him everything in Minneapolis. I can't wait."

"That will be a relief for poor Clarice, for a while at least," Emily said, chuckling.

Out of the corner of her eye, she spotted Mr. Ball leaning against the churchyard wall. She realized that she had been fooling herself about being calm and prepared for this meeting. She was not. Her belly was suddenly a mass of writhing snakes, and she feared she would not be able to utter a single word because her mouth was so dry. Even her palms were sweating, which was peculiarly disconcerting. She wasn't even able to make herself put one foot in front of the other, so she had to wait for him to come to her.

CHAPTER 23

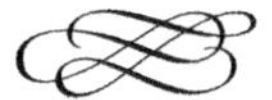

December 22, 1889, Iron Creek, Minnesota

As he made his way through the last remaining groups outside the church, Richard couldn't help thinking about the very pretty dress that Emily was wearing under her coat. He'd seen her from his pew in the back of the church during the service and was touched that she had chosen a dark blue gown to match her eyes even though he would not see it under her coat while they walked. She looked particularly lovely that morning, her cheeks flushed from the cold and a few tendrils escaping from her carefully pinned hair.

He wondered what she had been saying to Marta. The poor girl had looked most put out. But that wasn't why he was here. It didn't really matter to him. All that mattered was the girl in front of him.

"Good day to you, Miss Watson," he said, giving her a polite bow.

"And to you, Mr. Ball," she said. "How is your aunt? I have not been to the clinic since late Friday night. I do hope she is doing well."

"She actually spoke her first words yesterday," Richard said. "She was so proud of herself, though I can tell she is frustrated that she cannot tell us all off for fretting over her."

"She is a very independent woman," Emily said, clearly admiring his aunt's courage.

"She has had to be. With my uncle away so much, she not only ran her own household but also had to keep an entire fort's morale up. She is a woman of great fortitude."

"Yes, she is," Emily agreed. She glanced around and realized that they were the last people standing outside the church. "Shall we take that walk before we both freeze on the spot?"

"That would be a fine idea," he said, offering her his arm. They took the path to the side of the church that would lead them down to the creek again. Emily remembered the last time they had walked this path and the magnificent stag they had encountered. That had been such a strange day, one she often thought of. It had changed her entire life.

"We're hoping Aunt Mary will be able to come home on Christmas Eve, though the rooms are hardly suitable for an invalid," Richard said thoughtfully as their feet crunched into the snow that had fallen overnight. "I wish the house was ready. It would be much more practical for her to be there."

"It is unfortunate," Emily agreed. "It might seem a strange suggestion, but I could ask my father if the two of you might stay with us until your house is ready? I'm sure he'd be delighted to be of assistance. After all, the house is too big for the three of us, and there is a lovely big salon at the back that looks out onto the garden. There are wide doors, so if she were in a wheeled chair, like Mr. Cable's, she could enjoy some fresh air out on the porch, well wrapped up, of course."

"It would certainly be more suitable for her than my having to carry her up and down the stairs every time she wished to go out anywhere. But I couldn't leave her alone."

"Who said she would be alone?" Emily said. "There is a handsome room on the other side of the hall from mine. We could have the bed made up in there for you. I'd not expect you to come and go like a visitor. No, the place should be home for both of you, or not at all."

"Thank you. I shall ask her what she thinks," Richard said. "It is very kind of you. Are you sure you would want me to be in your home every single day?" He had tried his best to keep his tone light, teasing even, but he could see in her eyes that she knew he had asked a somewhat loaded question. He didn't expect her to answer.

"I should be happy to see you every day," she said softly.

"It would be like when we came here, on the train and at the hotel together."

"I enjoyed that, too," he admitted cautiously. She had agreed to come walking. He must not scare her away again. He had to remember to take things slowly, to give Miss Watson time. "I know we have not yet finished our walk, but I wondered if you would like to come and see the house with me tomorrow. Geoffrey wants my opinion on how to finish a few things. I have no idea what would be best. Such things are my dear aunt's favorite thing to worry herself over. Perhaps you would know better what she might like?"

She laughed, and Richard knew he had judged it just right. "I doubt that I have as exacting an eye as your aunt, but if you think I can be of assistance, I would very much like to see how work on your house is coming along."

"Are you working at the clinic?"

"I am, but I should be finished by ten o'clock as I will be there overnight. I may be a little sleepy, but I will be free all day after that."

"That must be hard," Richard said as they emerged from the trees and stepped onto the banks of the creek. The usually gushing waterway was strangely silent, its water frozen solid in the cold weather. They walked along the path toward the place they had picnicked last time. It was far too cold to stop moving this time. "Do you do many nights in a row, or do you all take it in turns to do one?

"I'm not sure I will ever get used to being up all night,

but it is part of the job when we have patients. Someone has to be there to take care of them. At the moment we all take turns, but once I am fully trained, we may start doing them for four days at once. It is easier, I think, to get used to it that way rather than switching back and forth all the time."

"Are you truly enjoying it as much as you seem to be?" He had seen how competent Miss Watson was before she came to Iron Creek, but every time he saw her in the clinic, she seemed to have learned so much more. "I know Nelly is pleased with how quickly you are learning everything."

"I am enjoying it," Miss Watson admitted. "It is not a career I ever considered before coming here. A girl like me isn't considered genteel enough to train as a nurse in a Boston hospital."

"It's funny that all the doors that were closed to you there would never have been so if they'd known whose daughter you truly were," Richard mused.

"Not necessarily funny. Given that my father was the black sheep of the family, I think it unlikely his name would have done me much good, even if he and my mother had been able to be together all along."

That was true enough. For a short while they walked without speaking. It was something Richard had rarely found comfortable, but he always did with Miss Watson. He didn't need to fill the silence with nonsense to hide his anxieties. She calmed him somehow, though being with her also made him as nervous as a man could ever be.

It was too cold for many birds or beasts to be about, but they occasionally caught sight of the imprints of a three-clawed talon in the snow, or the tiny pads of a paw. Miss Watson was always the one to spot them; her eyes were sharp as an eagle's. She stopped for a moment and looked around, her eyes wide with pleasure. Then, cautiously, she stepped out onto the ice of the creek. "Do you think it is frozen enough to hold me?"

"I think we are about to find out," Richard joked. "But at least it is shallow if you do fall in. You'd barely get up to your knees if you go through."

Fortunately, the ice held her. She walked slowly, cautiously, picking her way along the creek bed. Richard decided to take a chance and join her. He stepped onto the ice and waited for a moment to be sure it would hold his greater weight, then tried to follow her. It was harder than she had made it look, and he was soon flat on his backside, staring up at her giggling face.

"You've not done this before, have you?" she said, offering him her hand to help him back up.

"I think it wise if I get up without your kindly offered assistance," he said. "I fear I might bring us both down otherwise."

Richard managed to somehow get to his knees. Deciding he'd pushed his luck to its limits, he crawled to the bank and used its solidity to help get back to his feet. "I think I shall stay on snowy land," he said, turning back to her. She was still laughing but trying hard not to. It made her snort in a most unladylike manner, which made him laugh with her.

"How do you do that?" Richard asked her as she continued to move about on the ice.

"I used to skate, back in Boston. My mother had a pair of blades. They were her most treasured possession other than my father's watch. They were old and not sharp enough, really, but when the weather got cold and the lake in the park iced over, we'd go and skate, taking it in turns to strap those old blades to our boots." Her face was dreamy as she recalled those obviously happy times with her mother.

"We weren't often in places that had ice like this," Richard said as he helped her back up onto the bank. "Not until I went to university in Boston, of course. Though, I'm sure you'll agree that Boston was never as cold as it gets here."

"Not even close," Miss Watson said. "I used to think I knew what cold was until I moved here. I am more glad than I can tell you that my father can afford to buy me warm clothing and has such a well-built house."

"It is a beauty. Has he ever said anything much about it?"

"A little," Miss Watson said. "He had it built for the town, to show that they meant business. He gave it to the town, you know."

"He did? I'd not heard that."

"Yes, as a home for all mayors to come, he said. He

wanted to use the inheritance he got when his father died on something that would drive his parents wild."

"I can imagine that a civic building would not have been what they would have expected," Richard said, admiring Logan's generosity. "And yet his family does not know of that part, so if they were to see his house, they might think he had not left their ways behind him. It's very clever."

"The only person in town who knew was Mr. Graham, Nelly's husband."

"The man who was the attorney here before me," Richard said. "I have his records, so it would be likely that the documents pertaining to the donation are somewhere in my office."

They took the path that would lead them to the other end of town. This one went through what was probably a wild-flower meadow when it wasn't covered in a foot of snow. Miss Watson stopped for a moment, then bent down and picked up a handful of it. She rolled it into a ball, then pretended to throw it at him. "Shall we make a snowman?" she asked with a grin.

"I've never made one, I don't think," Richard said. "Why not? Show me what to do."

Miss Watson took her tight ball of snow and began to roll it around on the snow on the ground. It grew with each turn, and she carefully rotated it a little each time to ensure that it got bigger equally. "We need two large balls and a smaller one," she told him. "You can just heap up the snow together, but then your snowman will be gone as soon as there is the tiniest bit of sunshine. It is best to do it this way because the balls are more solid, more like ice than snow, so they melt more slowly."

Richard copied her, and soon they had two large balls. One was slightly smaller than the other, and Miss Watson told Richard to put that one on top of the larger one. She quickly made another, smaller ball, which Richard then placed on the very top.

"We need a scarf, some coal, and a carrot," she said.

Richard took off his own scarf and handed it to her. She wrapped it around the snowman's neck, then carefully formed a deep line on either side of the central ball, making it look like he had arms folded over his fat belly, then down the very middle of the bottom ball, to make legs. She heaped a little extra snow at the very bottom, shaping it to look like he was wearing heavy boots.

Standing back and watching her, Richard couldn't help but admire her efforts. The snowman was really coming alive. If only he had a face. "We should get back in the warm," he said. "I'll bring him back some eyes and a nose."

"I can make him a face," she said, clearly enjoying every minute of her play. Her gloves were sodden, but she didn't seem to notice as she quickly sculpted a smile, a nose, and two kind-looking eyes. "There," she said, standing back to admire her handiwork.

But once she had stopped moving, she began to notice

the cold again. Her teeth chattered. Richard peeled off her wet gloves and shoved them into his pockets, then ripped off his own and put them on her slender hands. They were far too big, but that didn't matter.

"We're going back now," he said firmly. She nodded, and they set off at a brisk pace. "Your father will kill me if I bring you home half frozen."

CHAPTER 24

Christmas Eve, 1889, Iron Creek, Minnesota

Emily had been lucky. Mr. Ball's swift action in getting her wet gloves off her hands and getting her home quickly had probably saved her from frostbite. Dr. Anna had scolded her when she learned of Emily's folly. But no harm had been done, and now Iron Creek had its own snowy guardian, watching for enemies coming from the creek. Emily had also found that thinking about Mr. Ball and their walk together helped to pass the time when she was alone in the clinic at night.

Nobody would need to be on duty in the clinic that night because Mrs. Ball was going home in the afternoon, just in time for Christmas. Though it would not be her own home. Logan had been delighted by the idea of having the Balls stay until their house was finished. He was particularly excited about the idea of having a big Christmas meal, turkey and all the trimmings, with everyone in the fancy dining room that he'd never once used since having the house built.

Emily helped Mary to get settled in a wheeled chair that Alec had made for her. It was just like Andrew Cable's.

"I am so grateful," Mrs. Ball said, mouthing each word slowly and carefully. Her speech was still a little slurred, and she had to think very carefully about how to say each word before she did so, but it was improving every day.

"We are just glad you are well enough to go home to be with your family for Christmas," Dr. Anna said with a smile.

"Now, you tell whoever is in charge of driving you to remember the brakes every time they step away from the chair," Alec warned her. "The last thing we want is you back in here because your chair ran away and caused an incident."

Mrs. Ball grinned. She looked as though she would rather enjoy a high-speed chase. "I promise," she said. "Merry Christmas to you and your lovely family."

Dr. Anna bent down and kissed her on the cheek, and Alec gave her a courtly bow, which made Mrs. Ball actually giggle. Then the bell over the door clanged loudly as Mr. Ball arrived. He was beaming.

"Ready, Aunt Mary?" he asked. She nodded, so he took the handles at the back of the chair and began to push her outside.

"A moment," Emily called out, hurrying to cover Mrs. Ball with another blanket. "Just in case."

Mr. Ball grinned at her, obviously pleased that she had learned her lesson enough to press it upon other people – being well wrapped up in a Minnesota winter was the only thing to do.

"I shall see you at home soon," Emily said. "Logan is waiting for you at the house. He is keen to get you both settled in. Dr. Anna wanted me to remind you that you need to hold the chair with the brakes whenever you stop. Just to ensure your aunt does not roll away and cause an incident!" Dr. Anna nodded her approval.

"Thank you," Mr. Ball said to everyone, but he gave Emily a special nod. She bit her lip as she watched him head down the street, using the ramps and walkways that Alec kept clear of snow so Andrew Cable could get around without needing assistance. It never stopped amazing Emily how everyone in the town went out of their way to help one another. If someone had tried to tell her about all the things Iron Creek did for all of its citizens, she would never have believed them. You had to be there to see it, to know that it was real, and to see that it all worked perfectly.

She did not have much to do once they were gone, but she and Nelly gave the clinic a thorough clean from top to bottom. When they were finished, everything sparkled and a large pile of dirty linens filled a basket by the door.

"I'll take them," Nelly said. "You go home and spend Christmas with your family."

"Who are you spending it with?" Emily asked.

"Oh, I'll be glad of a peaceful day to myself," Nelly said. "Don't you worry about me."

"Why not join us? For lunch, at least. We have far too much turkey. Logan bought a larger bird than five people could ever need. And Marta is a very fine cook."

"That is a tempting proposition. I think things at the bakery are even better since she got here, though I'd never say it to her or to Wes. They bring out the best in each other, that is for sure."

"Yes, they do," Emily agreed. "So, can I set you a place at the table? I know it would please Mrs. Ball to have her dear friend there with us."

"I'd be delighted," Nelly said.

"We'll see you at church, then you can come back with us?"

"Go home, Emily, before you invite the whole town to dinner," Nelly said with a warm smile. "You're a good girl."

At the house, Emily found a happy home. Mrs. Ball was overseeing Mr. Ball and Marta as they dressed the banister with evergreens.

"It looks very festive," Emily said, coming in and shutting the door quickly behind her. Once in the warm, she took off her coat and joined in the fun. Before long, the entire house smelled of pine branches, cinnamon, cloves, and orange. Mistletoe hung in every doorway, and holly was draped artfully on each mantel.

"I think I shall take a nap and leave you young folk to get the preparation for tomorrow's lunch underway," Mrs. Ball said slowly. "Richard, dear, would you mind taking me to my room?"

"Of course not," Richard said. He took his place at the back of the chair and wheeled her through to the back salon.

Marta led the way to the kitchen and picked up a large basket full of vegetables and placed it on the table. "We have a lot to do," she said with a smile, "so, roll up your sleeves and get your apron on."

Emily did just that, then she picked up a sharp knife and started to peel the potatoes.

"I still can't believe that he didn't ask you to marry him," Marta said as she started to slice them and drop them into a pot on the stove.

"We just went for a walk," Emily said. "It was lovely to not be discussing finding my father or anything else, just getting to know each other a little better."

"And you definitely like him?"

"I do."

"And you would say yes now, if he asked?"

"Marta, he'll be back at any moment. Now is the time to peel vegetables," Emily warned her. She wasn't yet ready to answer that question in her own mind, much less say it out loud.

Mr. Ball returned not long after. "So, how can I help?" he asked. He took off his jacket, rolled up his sleeves, and removed his tie.

Marta handed him a knife and the carrots. "You can peel and chop those in even rounds," she said.

He didn't argue. Nobody did. In the kitchen, Marta was most definitely in control. She kept them busy for a couple of hours, and by the end of it, Mr. Ball had convinced them both to call him Richard and been permitted to call them by their first names, too.

"Now, shoo," Marta said when the vegetables were done. "I have some things to do to finish off our supper tonight."

Emily took Richard into the parlor. "Would you like a drink?" she asked, moving toward her father's tray on the dresser, where three crystal decanters were filled with sherry, brandy, and whiskey.

"I must confess to rather enjoying a small sherry before dinner," Richard admitted. "I think it is because I came of age living with my aunt rather than my uncle. If he were here, he'd prefer a good bourbon."

Emily smiled and poured them each a small glass of sherry. They took their glasses and sat down beside the fire. "I am glad that we have a moment alone," she said. "I wanted to say thank you, again, for getting me home safely the other day. Dr. Anna saw how red and raw my hands were from the cold and gave me a lecture about frostbite."

"I hope you will take heed of her words," Richard said with a smile.

"It is easy to forget how cold you are. It is the strangest thing that you feel very warm when you are actually half frozen."

"I am glad we saved your fingers because I spoke to your father last night," Richard said. He reached into his pocket and pulled out a small jewelry box. "I asked for his blessing to ask you something I have asked before."

"You did?" Emily asked. "Goodness, no wonder I have barely seen him all day. No doubt he feared he might let your secret slip if he saw me. He is not very good at keeping secrets."

"I think he is very good at keeping secrets, just not from keeping good news from those he loves," Richard said gently.

"Yes, that is probably more what it is."

Richard opened the box to reveal a beautiful gold ring. The setting held a dark sapphire surrounded by tiny seed pearls. Emily gasped when he knelt on one knee before her.

"I did not do anything right last time, so I was determined to get everything right this time," he said, smiling up at her. "Dearest Emily, my life has been turned upside down and inside out since I met you. But I believe that it was our destiny to come together, to find your father, and to come here to a place where we can live happily without fear of what others might think. I love you with all my heart, and every moment I spend with you makes me more sure of that. Will you marry me?"

Emily bit her lip, shook her head, and felt tears begin to pour down her cheeks. "Yes," she whispered. "I would love to marry you."

"You're sure?" he asked. "You don't think anyone here will look down upon me for choosing the finest woman I've ever known – other than my aunt, of course." He grinned at her.

"I'm sure," she said. "You were right. Iron Creek is different. There are people here from all walks of life, some with money, others with almost none, yet everyone is wanted. Everyone is valued. And everyone here would do anything to help their neighbors."

"I shall cherish the fact that I was right, for I am sure that I will be forever wrong from now onwards," Richard said cheekily.

"Richard, I wanted to say yes last time, but I wasn't sure that your world would accept me and I wasn't sure that we knew each other well enough. I wasn't ready. In truth, I did not know who I was. It took coming here to learn that. Now I have work I love. I have a family again, and I have you. I have loved you from the start, but that is not enough for a marriage to work. My parents showed me that."

"We are not your parents."

"No, we are not. But their world was not so different from the one you lived in when you were in Boston."

"That is true enough," Richard acceded. He leaned toward her and pressed a kiss to her lips. "I am so glad I did not give up."

"So am I," Emily said.

"So are we," Marta, Logan, and Mrs. Ball said together, bursting into the room unable to wait any longer to congratulate them. In moments, Emily was in her father's arms and Marta was hugging Richard before he bent down and kissed his aunt, then shook Logan's hand. Emily hovered in front of Mrs. Ball. It felt a little strange to just kiss her or embrace her.

"Come here, child," the older woman said, reaching out her arms. "You must call me Aunt Mary now, for we are family. You have made my beloved Richard so happy." The two women embraced, and Aunt Mary held Emily's hand even when she stood back up. "This was my ring. Richard's uncle gave it to me when we were engaged."

"Thank you for entrusting it to me, and entrusting Richard to me, too," Emily said. "I'll take care of them both, I promise you that."

EPILOGUE

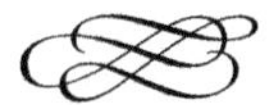

April 15, 1890, Iron Creek, Minnesota

Emily peeked through the door as her father caught his breath after the short walk. The church was full. She could see Harriet and Martyn, John and Graeme, Fiona and Evie being seated by Marta in the very front pew. Harriet was trying to argue, but Emily had told Marta to be sure they were right at the front. Harriet had become a second mother to her, and the Tolmans were her family. Finally, they seemed to accept that Marta was not to be budged and took their seats. Harriet looked around a little self-consciously as if she wished to apologize to whoever she might have displaced.

Not so long ago, Emily would have been the same. She'd never sat in the front row of a church. Such privileged places were for the wealthy in society, not the likes of her who might be lucky to even get a spot in a pew at all. Iron Creek truly was different that way. Her father had, of course, been allotted the front pew by the town, but he had confessed to Emily that he had only started to use that privilege once she and Marta had come to town. He was proud enough to want to show off his lovely daughter.

She turned to him now. "Are you ready, Papa?"

He looked at her, his eyes wide. "You called me Papa," he said, his eyes filling with tears.

"I did," she said. She pressed a kiss to his cheek and tucked her arm through his. "I am so glad that Richard found you."

"And I am glad that he brought you to me. I have so much to thank him for."

"You've offered him my hand in marriage," Emily said with a grin.

"I've barely got to know you, and already you'll be off."

"But I will only be at the old Bailey place," Emily reminded him. "And you are to come to dinner every Sunday. And Marta will be staying with you. She'll take good care of you."

"I am glad of that. She is an excellent cook, and I have come to think of her as another daughter."

"I think she would be glad to know that."

Emily fidgeted a little with her dress, straightened his tie, then smiled. "Shall we go in?"

"I suppose we should, or poor Richard will think you have jilted him at the altar," her father said, smiling through his tears. "I promised myself that I wouldn't cry, and then you went and called me Papa." He pulled out a handkerchief, blew his nose loudly, then wiped his eyes.

He offered her his arm and each of them took a handle of the double doors into the church, opening them wide. Richard was standing at the altar, handsome as always, his eyes full of love as they walked slowly toward him. Emily barely saw the other members of the congregation. All she could see was him. He smiled at her, then took her hand from her father and gave it an encouraging squeeze.

"You look lovelier than ever," he said as they stepped up toward the altar, where Father Michael from the church in Boston and Father Paul both stood smiling down at them.

The two priests shared the ceremony between them. As Emily spoke the words that would bind her to Richard forever, she couldn't help thinking about how much had changed for her. Less than a year ago, she had begun a search to find her father, hoping that he would be able to answer her questions. Because of that, she had met Richard, the man she loved with all her heart. The two of them had brought her here, to Iron Creek, where she had friends and a job that she adored. And shortly, they would open the doors of the home where they would raise a family and build a life together. She had to pinch herself, often, to remember that it hadn't all been a dream.

"You may kiss your bride," Father Michael said with a grin.

Richard didn't need to be told twice. He put his arms around Emily and pressed his lips to hers. For a moment, the rest of the world fell away, but then they heard the rapturous applause and whooping of their friends and family and broke apart giggling. Emily knew that her face must be beet red because her skin felt like fire.

"Thank you, Fathers," Richard said softly to the two priests.

"I am honored to have been invited," Father Michael said. "It is rather lovely to have been present for both your wedding and your mother's, Mrs. Ball." He beamed at Emily, whose face was still a little flushed.

"I am just glad that you could come, and that you brought my family with you," she said happily.

"They seem to feel a little out of place," Father Paul said. "Do they not usually attend church?"

"Not in the front pew," Emily said, grinning. "Boston is a little more formal about where the likes of us may sit."

"Not in my church," Father Michael said firmly. "Everyone is equal in the eyes of our Lord."

"Now, the pair of you must go. Enjoy your celebrations," Father Paul said. "Go with God."

"We will see you there, won't we?" Richard asked.

"Yes. I shall bring Father Michael along, as soon as we are finished here," he assured them.

Emily and Richard made their way down the aisle and out into the sunlight. Snowdrops bobbed their pretty heads along the sides of the path, and the daffodils would not be long in opening their pretty yellow trumpets. Blossoms were beginning to show on the trees, and the world felt new and fresh.

Richard stopped at the church gate, held Emily's hands in his, and looked into her eyes. "When we found out that my uncle had placed that advertisement, I was furious. Even though he was dead, he was still meddling in my life. But I cannot thank him enough. Everything that has happened since has made my life perfect. I love you, Mrs. Emily Ball."

"I love you, too, Mr. Richard Ball. I was so cheeky, sending that letter."

"It was destiny that you saw the advertisement and replied in that way. I barely even read the supposedly proper replies."

"And it was destiny that you came to Iron Creek and became friends with the Cables so you could actually meet my father when I believed the search was over."

"And now, it is destiny that we live happily ever after," he added with a cheeky wink.

"With perhaps the odd argument and difficult moment. Character comes from trials and tribulations," Emily corrected him. "Life would be terribly dull if everything worked out perfectly, wouldn't it?"

"As long as you are in my life, my life is perfect," Richard said, before placing a gentle kiss upon her lips.

The End

OTHER SERIES BY KARLA

Sun River Brides

Ruby Springs Brides

Silver River Brides

Eagle Creek Brides

Iron Creek Brides

Faith Creek Brides

CONNECT WITH KARLA GRACEY

Visit my website at www.karlagracey.com to sign up to my newsletter and get free books and be notified as to when my new releases are available.

Printed in Great Britain
by Amazon

22910408R00158